MIRANDA'S LAST STAND

Miranda's Last Stand

Gloria Whelan

■ HARPERCOLLINS*PUBLISHERS*

http://www.harperchildrens.com

Library of Congress Cataloging-in-Publication Data
Whelan, Gloria.
    Miranda's last stand / Gloria Whelan.
        p.   cm.
    Summary: Because the Sioux had killed her papa at the
Battle of Little Bighorn, eleven-year-old Miranda struggles
with her mama's prejudice and her own experiences with
Indians in the Wild West Show.
    ISBN 0-06-028251-7. – ISBN 0-06-028252-5 (lib. bdg.)
    1. Buffalo Bill's Wild West Show–Juvenile fiction.
[1. Buffalo Bill's Wild West Show–Fiction.   2. Prejudices–
Fiction.   3. Little Bighorn, Battle of the, Mont., 1876–
Fiction.   4. Dakota Indians–Fiction.   5. Indians of North
America–Great Plains–Fiction.]   I. Title.
PZ7.W5718Mj   1999   99-21189
[Fic]–dc21   CIP

Typography by Alison Donalty
    1   2   3   4   5   6   7   8   9   10   ❖   First Edition

For Joe,
who made the trip with me

MIRANDA'S LAST STAND

CHAPTER ONE

In 1876, when I was two years old, Papa rode out with General Custer to fight Sitting Bull and his Sioux warriors and never came back. General Custer and the men of the Seventh Cavalry bravely attacked the Indians at the Little Big Horn River. Papa and every other soldier in the Seventh Cavalry was killed.

Mama has told me, "Those were terrible days, Miranda. Everywhere you looked there was black. We all wore black. There were black wreaths on the doors. Through the open windows you could hear the crying of the soldiers' wives. In the barracks the soldiers vowed revenge on the hateful Chief Sitting Bull and his evil warriors."

Mama had made a painting of the Seventh Cavalry as they marched across the parade ground. It hung in our sitting room, and I looked at it every day.

The figure of Papa on his horse was smudged. When I was little, I used to climb up onto a chair to touch him.

At the head of the mounted soldiers was General Custer with his long red-gold hair, his black hat with the brim turned up, and his sleeves heavy with gold braid. He was riding his favorite horse, Vic. Strung out behind the cavalry were the artillery, the cannons, and the Gatling guns. Then came the long line of pack mules and covered wagons carrying supplies for the soldiers' journey.

Mama had painted in the wives of the soldiers. Some of them were holding up babies so they could see their fathers march off. In the picture there were children with flags made of handkerchiefs tied to sticks. There were children drumming on pots. Mama said the band was playing "The Girl I Left Behind Me."

After Papa was killed, we had no place to go. Many of the cavalry wives went back to their families. When I was older, I asked Mama, "Why didn't we go and live with your mama and papa?" I had never met them, but their picture was on her dresser, and each Christmas a letter would come with their address on the back of the envelope. Like us, they lived in the Dakota Territory. Their home wasn't far from Fort Lincoln, where we lived. When the letter arrived, Mama would go into our bedroom and close the door to read it. When she came out, her eyes were red from crying. She never explained why the letter made her cry or why her parents hadn't taken us in. "I'll tell you when you're older, Miranda" was all she said.

After Papa's death the new commander of the fort offered Mama a place on Laundresses' Row, which is what the fort calls the string of little houses where the laundresses live. Mama accepted. We moved from a large officer's house into two cramped rooms.

Laundresses were paid seventy-five cents a month for each enlisted man's clothes they washed, and a dollar for washing the clothes of an officer. Mama disappeared into a froth of soapsuds. A great soiled heap of clothes came daily in a wagon. The clothes were sent back fresh and folded. From the beginning I helped—folding when I was small, pinning up when I grew tall enough to reach the clothesline. I could tell the seasons by the drying of the laundry. In the spring the wind whipped the sheets into great white ghosts. In summer the sheets were a snowstorm bleaching on the grass. In fall we had to shake off the leaves as we gathered in the laundry. In winter if we hung out, we had stiff boards to bring in.

As I grew older, I tired of the endless heaps of laundry. When I could slip away, I explored the fort. Every part of it became familiar to me. On one side of a large square were the commander's home and the officers' houses where we had once lived. I used to stand looking at them, imagining what it would be like to have my own room, and a porch with roses climbing up the pillars, and a swing to rock on.

Across the square from the officers' houses were the barracks for the enlisted men. You could smell their tobacco smoke and hear the thump of their boots as they pulled them off and their sighs of relief as they stretched their toes after a hard day's marching. There was a hospital for sick soldiers and a guardhouse for bad ones. Flames danced all day long at the smithy, where the horses were shoed. There was an icehouse. When I poked my head into it in the summer, it felt cold as winter.

I especially loved to visit the corral and see Comanche. All the soldiers and all their horses had died at the Battle of the Little Big Horn, except for one horse, Comanche. When Comanche was discovered still alive after the battle, he had twenty bullets in him. When he was well enough, they brought him back to the fort. I went to see him every day, bringing him cubes of sugar, which he plucked from my fingers with his large teeth. He was golden brown with a dark mane and tail and gentle dark eyes. Sometimes I whispered questions to him, but there were no answers. "How I wish he could tell me what happened!" I said to Mama. "He must have been close to Papa when Papa was killed by the Indians."

Mama shook her head and said, "Miranda, it's a blessing Comanche can't talk."

Everyone at the fort loved Comanche. No one was allowed to ride him, but every time there was a special ceremony at the fort, Comanche was led out with great honor to parade with the cavalry. When Mama saw Comanche saddled up, she said, "No one at Fort Lincoln or anywhere in this country will ever forget the Battle of the Little Big Horn."

My favorite day was Sunday, when I had Mama all to myself and no laundry. After church Mama and I walked in the fields around the fort. In the spring the fragrance of the wild roses hung in the air. In the fall the buckbrush berries turned white and the buffalo berries red. When I was old enough to walk long distances, Mama and I packed apples and bread and cheese, and we'd wander for miles over the hills or along the Missouri River. Mama would stand with her face turned up to the sun and wind. "I must get the soap and the dampness out of me, Miranda," she'd say.

Once we came to a field with many stone circles. "Who could have put them there?" I asked.

Mama shuddered. "Indians. Those stones kept the wind from blowing their tepees loose."

"Indians lived here?" The thought was exciting, and I wanted to learn more.

But Mama had a sharpness in her voice when she spoke, and though I had done nothing wrong, I felt I was being scolded. "Come away quickly, Miranda," she said.

Much as Mama disliked Indians, we saw them every day. At the fort there were always Indians. The Crows scouted for the soldiers. Even though they fought on our side, Mama would turn away when she saw one. I tried to hate all the Indians as well. Still, I could not stop looking at their feathered headdresses, their brightly colored clothes, and their decorations made of silver and bone and the teeth of grizzly bears. I did not see how Mama could keep from painting the Indians. They were always pleasant to me, smiling and waving when they caught me watching them. Sometimes I waved back, but sometimes I didn't, afraid Mama would see.

Each time the soldiers celebrated another victory over the Indians, Mama rejoiced. "Indians are all alike," she said. "They are all our enemy."

CHAPTER TWO

Our lives changed again the day Mama got the letter. It was a month after my tenth birthday. The printing on the envelope was thick and sharp like sticks. Mama held the envelope in her hand a long time before she opened it. Her hands shook as she read the letter. At last she cried, "Oh, Miranda, my mama and papa are gone. The lawyer says Papa died two months ago and Mama's heart gave out last week." Mama put her head in her hands. I saw her shoulders shaking. She whispered, "I never asked Papa's forgiveness. I was very wicked."

I was frightened by Mama's sobs. I crept closer to her and put my arms around her. "Forgiveness for what, Mama?" I asked.

Mama wiped her eyes and looked at me. "I suppose you are old enough now, Miranda." She sank down on the sofa and drew me to her. Taking my hands in hers, she began to speak quietly. "There was a Fourth of July celebration for the Seventh Cavalry in Bismarck. I remember fireworks and dancing. I went to the celebration with my parents. I met your papa there, and we fell in love. We wrote to one another. When we wanted to get married, my parents said Papa and I were too young. I was just seventeen and Papa was twenty. But my mind was set." Mama's face turned stubborn. Her lips were thin and straight, like a twig. "When we eloped, my father disowned me. He was a God-fearing man, Miranda, but he had none of the Lord's forgiveness. My mama relented. Each Christmas she wrote to me and sent me money. She begged me to tell my papa I was sorry, but I couldn't bring myself to put down the words. It's a terrible thing not to forgive, Miranda. Your grandpa would not forgive me, and I was too proud to ask. Now it's too late."

I hung on to Mama. It was the saddest, most romantic tale I had ever heard. Her father might have forgiven her, I thought, but Mama would not have forgiven her father.

After a moment Mama said, "But, Miranda, there

was something more in the letter." Some of the sadness had left her face.

"What is it, Mama?" I asked.

"What little money my papa had was used for the funerals and to pay off debts, but the farm was left to you, Miranda. It's free and clear, and it's all yours."

"Mine! A farm?" I could hardly keep my feet on the ground. "Oh, Mama, when can we see it? Can we go there and live?"

Mama shook her head. "I'm afraid not, Miranda. We wouldn't have anything to live on until we had crops to sell."

"But can't we at least see it?" I begged. I was already imagining the farm, but I didn't want to make up something that might not be there. I didn't want to be disappointed.

The following Saturday we learned that a wagon was going to Bismarck for supplies. The driver agreed to take us to the farm, which was on the way, and to pick us up on his return. It was early in June, and the day was warm and windless. I kept asking Mama how much farther it was. It seemed like we would never get there. The cicadas' shrill cries were like pins sticking me. With few trees for shade along the road, I grew hot. Trees in Dakota are scarce.

We had been traveling for two hours when Mama called to the sergeant who was driving the wagon to stop. Mama jumped out of the wagon, and the sergeant lifted me down and waved good-bye to us. In the distance I could see a small white farmhouse. The wagon trail to the farmhouse had grown over. Mama and I made our way through tall grass, Mama walking slowly and me running as fast as I could, scaring up grasshoppers. It was my own house I was running to. I couldn't get there fast enough. There was a single cottonwood tree and an overgrown garden where lilacs and forget-me-nots bloomed. There was a patch of rhubarb with great leaves like elephant ears and an asparagus bed that was starting to fern out.

The house was deserted. The porch sagged, and the roof was in need of shingles. I peered into a window and saw a sitting room with a sofa and a couple of chairs. Quickly, I ran to the other windows. There was a kitchen, and two small bedrooms. I was sure the house was waiting just for me.

"Mama," I whispered, "is this house really mine?"

Mama didn't hear me. She was looking at everything. "I remember the smell of the lilacs and how I could hear the leaves on the cottonwood rustle at night," she said. A key to the house had come with the letter. Now Mama handed it to me. My hand was shaking so, I could hardly fit it into the lock. The key turned, and the door opened. Inside, it smelled musty and closed off. We opened the windows to let in the June air. Mama showed me where her room was. Her narrow bed was still there, and on her dresser there were a comb and brush and mirror. When I picked up the brush, I saw strands of Mama's golden hair.

In the kitchen Mama told me how she had sat at the table and shelled peas and how she had helped her mama preserve wild blackberries. "Oh, Miranda, how I wish I had made my peace." She slumped down on a kitchen chair and buried her face in her hands.

I put my arms around her and felt her warm tears against my cheek. It was terrible that she was so sad and I was so happy. I tried to stand still, but I couldn't stop myself. Soon I was peeking into the rooms. If we lived here, I would have a room for my own. When I had looked and looked, I went back to Mama. She was smiling at me.

"When can we move here, Mama?"

"Not until I find a way to save enough money to fix up the house. I'm afraid Mama and Papa let it go.

And we'll need money to buy seed. I've been think-ing—the fort's in need of fresh vegetables: corn and cabbage, berries and apples. The soldiers are sicken-ing with scurvy for want of them. All they get to eat is hardtack and baked beans. We could supply vege-tables and fruit. We wouldn't need much land for that, and if we could hire someone to plow the fields, you and I could farm the land. But to come by enough money to do all of that would take a long time."

I sighed, not knowing how I could wait even another day to escape Laundresses' Row. "At least can we come and visit the farm sometimes?" I asked.

Mama seemed as anxious to do that as I was. "Whenever I can find time from the laundry," Mama promised, "and a wagon comes this way."

I already felt at home. Yellow butterflies were tan-gled in the lilacs. Two squirrels were chasing each other around the trunk of the cottonwood tree. Nearby we could hear a creek's murmur. Mama and I settled on the bank of the creek and took off our shoes and stockings. We splashed our feet in the cold water, scaring up a muskrat. He looked so startled, Mama laughed and laughed, and then she hugged me.

"I think the house is my mama and papa's for-giveness, Miranda," she said.

꩜

The very next day Mama printed a sign and put it up in our window: PAINTINGS FOR SALE. PORTRAITS OF MEN, WOMEN, AND CHILDREN, PAINTED FOR A SMALL FEE. Hanging on our walls were paintings Mama had done over the years, pictures of the fort and soldiers on their horses and the Dakota countryside in winter and summer. Now Mama put prices on the paintings. She put no price on the painting of Custer riding out.

Many of the soldiers were anxious to send like-nesses of themselves to their mothers and fathers and sweethearts. They sat bolt upright, staring straight ahead while Mama sneaked time from the laundry to paint their portraits. Our little house smelled of var-nish and turpentine.

When she counted the money she had made with her painting, Mama's shoulders sagged and she bit her lip. "I don't see how I'll ever get enough money, Miranda. We daren't leave the fort until we have enough to live on for a year while our crops grow. And if there's a bad year with grasshoppers or hail or drought, I must have something put by."

On the days we spent at the farm, Mama busied herself fixing up the farmhouse while I explored the land. Because it was ours, I began to look hard at it, and I found it wasn't only ours after all. Green and black beetles traipsed all over it. Prairie dogs popped up from a hundred holes to stare at me. I discovered swifts in our chimney, and a groundhog's burrow under our porch. I scared up a dappled bird with a dandelion-yellow breast and a black half-moon at its throat—a meadowlark. Everywhere I looked, something was there before us. I wondered how they felt about our coming. When we moved into the house and began to work the land, where would they all go? I remembered the time when we had had no place to call our own, and I felt sorry for all the creatures.

One afternoon I waded the narrow ribbon of creek, feeling the current pull the sand from under my bare feet. I stubbed my toe against a stone. When I reached down for it, I found it was an Indian arrowhead. For a moment, curious, I held it in my hand. Indians must have lived here. But as I looked at the sharpened edges, I thought how just such an arrowhead might have killed Papa. I dropped it and ran back to Mama.

The fall came, and the leaves from the cotton-wood dropped onto the porch of the cottage. In November flakes of snow fell out of a clear blue sky, but the meadowlark was still there, silent on a bare branch. With the winter, our visits to the farmhouse were at an end. But in my heart I never left our farm, for all my thoughts stayed there. I planned how I would arrange my little room and how there would be a vase of lilacs on my dresser.

By the end of March the blizzards had stopped, and any snow that fell melted as it touched the ground. Fort Lincoln was hidden in mist as the warming air settled over the Missouri's cold water. Mama and I were planning our first visit to the farm when the commander of the fort summoned Mama to come and see him. "I can't think what the commander wants with me," Mama said. "With fewer soldiers stationed here, it might be they have less need for laundresses, but that wouldn't be something for the commander to bother himself over." With a heavy heart Mama put on her best dress and left for the commander's house.

I watched Mama walk across the field and disappear into the mist. Even though I knew the money

Mama earned from doing the laundry put meat and bread on our table, after all those years of dirty clothes and soapsuds, I almost wished the commander would dismiss Mama. Our hands were raw from the lye in the soap, and I was sick of the stink of dirty laundry. I would willingly have gone to our little farmhouse and starved to death there.

When Mama returned, she looked bewildered. "Miranda, the strangest thing has happened. The commander told me a cavalry soldier at the fort has gone to join something called Buffalo Bill's Wild West Show. This season's show opens in Chicago in May. It will travel all over the country. Buffalo Bill Cody, who owns the show, is looking for someone to paint scenery and posters. The soldier had some of my paintings with him, and now Mr. Cody wants me to come and work for him. The pay would be five times what I am making here."

I held my breath. "You wouldn't leave me, would you, Mama?"

"Of course not, Miranda. I wouldn't dream of going anywhere without you."

"What about our farm? What would happen to it?"

"We would leave in the spring and be back by fall. I believe this work would give us enough money to move to the farm."

"We could live there!" I began to think the Wild West Show a good idea. "But who is Mr. Cody?"

"Mr. Cody is a fine man. He fought against the Sioux and defeated them. It would be an honor to be employed by him. Miranda, shall we do it?"

For an answer I threw my arms around Mama.

CHAPTER THREE

We said good-bye to the farm and to everyone at the fort. Although it was late April, there were still a few rags of snow on the hills, but at the farm the rhubarb shoots were pushing up. I was sorry we would not be there to see the cottonwood tree leaf out or the lilacs bloom.

On the day we began our long journey to Chicago, I was in a state of hold-your-breath excitement until I saw the worry on the faces of those who had come to say good-bye. From their expressions I understood for the first time how far we were going. As the wagon carried us and our trunks away, I looked over my shoulder at the fort that had been our home for so many years. It grew smaller and smaller until it was not there anymore.

In Bismarck we boarded the steamship for our

trip down the Missouri to Omaha. Once I saw the ship's great paddle wheel turn and the smoke come billowing out of the chimney and heard the whistle blowing, my excitement returned. I clung to the railing of the ship for dear life, as if the steamship were a magic carpet that would take me on a ride to some far kingdom. And indeed the whole voyage was magic, for we got to see not only Dakota but bits of Nebraska and Iowa as well.

At the beginning of our trip there were only long stretches of empty land, and sometimes a fort with its watchtower and American flag. Once we saw a long file of Indians. The Indians were bent under heavy packs. They looked as if they were making a journey they did not wish to make. Unlike other travelers, who would stop to wave at the steamship, the Indians did not even look at us. I wondered how the Indians felt about the large steamships that were bringing so many people to claim the land.

"Where do you think they are going?" I asked Mama. She only shrugged and looked away from the Indians, but I couldn't stop wondering what would happen to them.

As the days passed, the empty spaces along the

shore turned into farms and towns. I'd had no idea the country was so big.

Mama kept hold of my hand. "We are traveling so far, Miranda. I only hope I have done the right thing," she fretted.

I began to worry, too, but in Omaha we boarded the train that would take us to Chicago. I had never ridden in a train. Its wailing whistle and the clatter of its wheels chased my worry away. The towns, which had been so stretched out on the Missouri River, began to come closer together. The train would pull up to a station, gnashing and roaring and shaking like a wild horse. There would be a town, with its church and school, its stores and flour mill. Sometimes the streets were ankle deep with mud. Sometimes there were logs or planks put down for people to walk on.

What I loved best of all was night on the train. For miles everything was dark and then, suddenly, from the train window, I would see a farm all by itself, its windows gold with candlelight. At first those houses looked lonely out there in the darkness; then I remembered that we were really the lonely ones. The people in the houses were home.

As we got closer to Chicago, the towns grew

larger. There was the smell of coal fires, and factories with tall chimneys giving off great puffs of smoke. When we finally stepped off the train in Chicago, the city exploded around us. The buildings were so high, they cut off the sun. I had never imagined so many people and carriages and houses all in one place. "Mama," I whispered, "what if we get lost here?"

Mama took hold of my hand and squeezed it. I guessed she was as frightened as I was.

I had been a little afraid of meeting Mr. Cody. I had heard many stories at Fort Lincoln of how Mr. Cody had avenged the death of Custer and the Seventh Cavalry by riding against Chief Yellow Hand. After he killed the chief, he cried, "First scalp for Custer!" He sent the chief's scalp, all packed in a little box, back to Mrs. Cody. What must she have thought upon opening the box!

I was relieved to find that Mr. Cody appeared a kindly man. He was there to collect us the moment we stepped from the train, greeting us with a warm smile and welcoming words. "I'm glad to meet you, mam," he said to Mama, "and you, little lady. We're happy to have you join our family." He had flowing black wavy hair, a mustache, and chin whiskers in a style Mama called an imperial. He wore a fringed buckskin jacket and a wide-brimmed hat. His outfit set him apart from the city's black-suited men.

A Mr. Bill Racher drove the carriage. He was tall and thin and so quiet he seemed like all the words had been squeezed out of him. He smiled at us but said nothing. The carriage was drawn by a pair of matched gray horses, their manes and tails braided. They looked high-strung; the whites of their eyes showed, and they pawed restlessly at the ground, anxious to be off. Mr. Cody helped Mama and me into the carriage. There was a flourish in all he did, like the curlicues people put into their writing.

Inside the carriage he turned to me. I held my breath, but he only said, "So you're Miranda. The sun shining on your hair puts me in mind of a field of Dakota wheat." As he looked at me, his face clouded over as if he were looking at someone else. A sad look. "How old are you, Miranda?"

"Eleven, sir."

"Near the age of my daughter, Ora."

"Is she with the show, sir?" Someone to be a friend.

"She died last year."

Mama put her hand softly on Mr. Cody's arm and then, embarrassed at her boldness, quickly took it away. I didn't think Mr. Cody minded. I made myself very sad by picturing Ora, pale and still, in a white dress, lying in a coffin with her hands crossed over her chest and flowers all about her.

As we drove along, there were shouts of "Buffalo Bill!" Buffalo Bill is what everyone called Mr. Cody. Painted on our carriage in big letters for all to see was BUFFALO BILL'S WILD WEST SHOW. Mr. Cody tipped his hat and smiled. He seemed to like the shouts, and after a bit his sadness disappeared. For myself, I did not know how I would ever live long enough to take in such a huge city.

On our trip from Dakota I had seen the busyness of cities through the train window, but in Chicago we were a part of it. Mama and I held hands. Hard. I thought there were more buildings than anyone could need. There were parks and wide boulevards where carriages and wagons dashed by, nearly colliding with us. Clanging streetcars went jerking along. It was a hornets' nest of people. There were women in elegant dresses and men with walking sticks and high hats.

"You won't see many wooden buildings," Mr. Cody said. "Just fourteen years ago the whole town burned down; thousands of houses went up in smoke. People ran into the lake to save themselves. Now what you have is a city of brick and stone that fire can't get to."

It was May, but a chill wind blew off the lake, rumpling the small, soft new leaves on the trees. With so much to confuse me, the nearness of the lake was a comfort. I had studied the map. To make Dakota a little closer, I began to imagine how I could build a little boat and sail it on Lake Michigan all the way up to Green Bay. From there I could cross Lake Winnebago and float along the maze of rivers until I reached the Mississippi. From the Mississippi I could get to the Missouri. Even from Chicago, I could find my way back to our farmhouse.

While I was daydreaming my way back to Dakota, Mr. Cody was talking to Mama about the show. "What we want, mam, is for you to paint a backdrop of Wyoming. I have some pictures here to give you an idea or two." More real than the pictures were his words. It was as if he had seen the country just yesterday and could see it still. "You start out with the hills, but before you know it there are the mountains. They are as high as you can imagine and then twice again as high, with snow on the tops winter and summer. In the valleys there are the rivers, the Platte and the Yellowstone and . . ." I think he was going to say "the Little Big Horn," but he had surely heard about Papa being killed there. Giving Mama a quick glance, he hurried on. "You've never seen such rivers, wild and clear as glass, and so full of fish you could just about reach in and grab them. You'll want to paint in some elk," he said eagerly. "Make them big and strong-looking, and put in a sly, slinking coyote or two, and maybe wolves running after a deer." Like me, he was imagining his way out of the city.

We came to the West Side Driving Park. "This is the home of the Wild West Show for the next week," Mr. Cody said. Stretched out as far as I could see was a village of tents, hundreds of them. There were small tents and tents as large as a barracks. There were people everywhere. I saw stables for horses and pens of buffalo and a whole menagerie of strange animals. I could hardly take it all in. I had never expected anything so big. I half wanted to run off and look at the animals, and I half wanted to hang on to Mama, afraid I would be lost among all those people.

Mr. Cody pointed to one of the small tents. "That's where you'll be living, mam." Mama looked surprised. "It's not fancy," Mr. Cody said, "but we'll do our best to make it comfortable for you." For myself, I was excited at the thought of living in a tent and anxious to see inside our strange new home.

Near the tents was a circle of tepees, each with its bristly topknot of sticks. "You have Indians in the show, Mr. Cody?" Mama's voice was brave, but I felt her hand tighten around mine.

"Oh, indeed, mam. We have cowboys and Mexicans and soldiers, and we have eighty Indians, all fine warriors."

Mama looked shocked, but I was curious about the Indian village, wondering if I would have a chance to see it up close.

"When we opened the show here on Sunday," Mr. Cody said, "forty thousand people bought tickets. You have to have Indians, mam. That's part of what the people come for. I do it for other reasons as well. It gives the Indians a paying job when many of them are going hungry. And they like traveling with the show. Instead of being cooped up on their reservations, they get to see something of the world."

Mr. Cody left us to settle into our tent. Mama stood for a moment looking over to the circle of tepees. "I hadn't counted on Indians, Miranda," she said. "Still, we won't have to have anything to do with them."

I did not see how that could be, with so many Indians close by, but I said nothing to Mama.

It was dim inside the tent, the only light coming in from the tent flap. There was the smell of new canvas. The tent was furnished with two folding chairs, a table, and two cots. There was a stand with a pitcher and a washbowl.

"Look, Mama," I said, "someone has filled the pitcher with water for us." The water standing ready made me feel welcome.

Mama opened one of our trunks and began to make a home. She spread a paisley shawl, her last gift from Papa, over a chair. She laid her hooked rug on the floor so that it looked like a small blue lake. The flying-geese quilt she placed on my bed. I lay down on the cot and then sat in the chair. I splashed water on my face and tidied my hair, looking in the small mirror that hung over the washstand.

At the foot of my bed was my trunk with my clothes, my lesson books, and a wooden horse Papa had carved for my first birthday. In Mama's trunk was her book of Mr. Shakespeare's plays. My name, Miranda, comes from one of the plays, *The Tempest.* Mama says that in the play Mr. Shakespeare means for the character, Miranda, to represent all that is good and pure. I often wished Mama had picked a name that wasn't so hard to live up to.

Mama propped a drawing she had made of Papa on the table. He was serious and handsome in his uniform. I always thought of Papa as he was in that drawing, handsome and dashing.

I felt myself wanting something, something that was missing in the tent. "We don't have a window, Mama."

Mama thought for a minute. Then she got out her paints and painted a window on the back wall of the tent. First she filled in a blue sky and then she sketched a tree with cardinals and bluebirds and goldfinches. She painted the birds red, blue, and gold. When she finished, Mama smiled at me. "It's not the farm, Miranda, but it will have to do."

Early the next morning Mr. Cody came to tell Mama she could begin painting the large canvas backdrop of Wyoming. "There are some children near Miranda's age traveling with the show," Mr. Cody said. "Why don't I take her over to meet them? Your girl can watch the show in their company this afternoon."

"That's very kind, Mr. Cody." Mama was already busy looking over her paints and brushes. From the way she caught her lower lip between her teeth, I could tell she was nervous about making the backdrop. Mama is always nervous before she begins a picture. She once told me, "I'm afraid while I'm sleeping all my cleverness will disappear. My painting is so close to my dreaming, Miranda, I worry it will go away like my dreams do."

I followed Mr. Cody out of the tent. To my surprise he headed toward the Indian village. Before we got there, three Indian children ran toward us. There were two girls and a boy. The older girl wore a summer dress with buckskin leggings underneath. The younger girl was in a tattered party dress with ruffles. The boy had on a buckskin tunic over leggings. His long black hair was held back by a beaded headband.

"Here are some friends for you, Miranda," Mr. Cody said. "The four of you can get acquainted." He strode off, leaving me in the middle of the three Indians. I stared at them with no thought for manners. They stared back at me. All I could think was that Mama would be very angry with me if I made friends with the Indians.

Finally the older girl said, "I'm Quick Fox, and my sister is Small Snow. My brother is Young Wolf."

Quick Fox, who looked to be my age, was slim, with two long black braids snaking down her back. Her face was a perfect oval. Her eyes were the color of brown stones shining in water. She was very handsome, and with her chin tilted up and her easy words, she seemed very sure of herself. "Small Snow is six," Quick Fox said. I had to smile at the roly-poly dumpling of a girl with a moon face and fat dimpled hands. "Young Wolf is thirteen," Quick Fox added. Her brother looked at me with watchful brown eyes, as if he were peering out of some hidden burrow or tree hollow.

I knew that Mama would not want me to stay. I was about to find my way back to our tent when

Quick Fox took hold of my hand in a friendly way and pulled me after her. "Hurry," she said. "The Grand Entry is beginning."

I stopped thinking about Mama. After all our days spent cooped up in trains, I was glad to be running. The park was overflowing with people. I heard lively marching music. We squeezed past the ticket takers, who gave Quick Fox a friendly wave. She pushed a tunnel for me through the crowd and dragged me right to the front row.

"You want a good view for your first time," she said. "I will tell you the name of everyone."

I glanced nervously around to see if the people near us thought it strange for me to be with Indians, but they paid us no mind. All their attention was on the opening parade, which was just starting. Leading the Grand Entry was a cowboy band. They made their music with drums and every kind of horn: trumpets, cornets, trombones, and bugles. Behind the band came Mr. Cody riding on his horse. So wild a cheer went up, a king might have been riding by. Next, a girl or a young woman, I couldn't tell which, rode by on a big white horse. Her hair was in long curls, and a gun was slung over her saddle. The cheers grew louder.

"That's Annie Oakley," Small Snow told me. "She can shoot better than anyone, even Mr. Cody."

Behind Annie Oakley rolled a stagecoach painted bright yellow and marked with the words U.S. MAIL. It was drawn by six mules. Quick Fox said, "That's the Deadwood coach. Mr. Nelson is driving it. That coach used to carry the mail between the Black Hills and Cheyenne. It was robbed all the time."

"*We* ride in it now," Young Wolf said in a proud voice.

I wondered what he meant at first, but thought no more about it when the parade continued. Cowboys twirled lariats, spinning circles fast as tornadoes. Mounted cavalry officers, wearing helmets with brass peaks, galloped by. The Stars and Stripes fluttered from its standard. Mexican horsemen with bushy mustaches, and big hats with pointed crowns and brims big as turkey platters, rode by. Then came the Indians on their horses, riding six abreast. They wore feathers in their hair, and their faces were bright with war paint. I started to pull away from Quick Fox. She must have seen that I was afraid, for she said, "Our people only dress like that for the show." Last of all was a herd of huge, shaggy buffalo.

I didn't know where to look first. It was all new. I had a million questions for Quick Fox. I was so mesmerized by everything, I almost forgot I was sitting with Indian children.

The show started off with the cowboy band playing "The Star-Spangled Banner." Next came Annie Oakley. She skipped lightly into the arena with her long curls bouncing and her short pleated skirt flicking out. Her leggings had little pearl buttons sewn all down the sides. There were embroidered flowers on her skirt and a fringe along its hem. She waved her wide-brimmed hat and blew kisses into the audience. The crowd whooped and blew kisses back, even the grown men.

"Who is the man with Annie Oakley?" I asked Quick Fox. He was handsome, with black hair and a mustache and fine brown eyes.

"That's Annie's husband, Frank Butler. He married Annie after she beat him shooting. She hit nine hundred forty-three out of a thousand glass balls. They always start out with Annie. She is so dainty, her shooting doesn't scare anyone. All the people see is a pretty little girl shooting a gun. After that, gunfire doesn't scare them so much."

Mr. Butler stood by a table covered with Annie's guns. He began to throw glass balls up in the air, and Annie shot them down. The balls glittered in the sun like soap bubbles before they shattered in midair. A hundred were thrown up and ninety-eight shot down.

"She could shoot them all," Quick Fox whispered, "but she misses some so people don't think there's a trick to it."

Annie Oakley shot with her right hand, then with her left hand. Mr. Butler threw up two balls at once, and she shot one, twirled around, and shot the second. She shot with her rifle upside down. She shot standing backward, looking into a mirror. She shot glass balls with feathers in them so that when the balls broke, the feathers exploded into the air. All the while she was shooting, Annie was smiling at the audience as if she shared a secret with them.

"Now it is our turn," Quick Fox said. "You can be in the show too." She tugged at my arm, but I hung back. "Come," she coaxed. "We must get into the coach."

It was all happening so quickly, I didn't know what I should do. I let her pull me to where the stagecoach was waiting, off to the side.

Mr. Nelson grinned at us. He had a round face with red cheeks and friendly blue eyes. You could see from the stately way he held the reins that he was proud to be driving six such fine mules. The Indian children threw on cloaks and hats. Some cowboys were putting on dresses and bonnets and getting inside the coach. Quick Fox explained in a rush, "There aren't any white ladies or children in the show, so they use the cowboys and us. We keep our hats over our heads so they can't tell we're Indians." Quick Fox climbed into the coach and pulled me up the high steps after her. The inside of the coach was all red velvet. I felt like a princess.

As the coach rolled out into the park, a great cheer went up. Suddenly Indians on ponies galloped toward us. The Indians' faces and bodies were painted red and black. They were whooping and hollering. Their rifles and arrows were pointed right at us. I covered my eyes with my hands. I was too scared to breathe. For one horrible minute I knew what Papa must have felt when Sitting Bull's warriors rode against him, and I screamed with all my might.

Mr. Nelson called, "That's a nice loud scream, girl. Stick your head out the window of the coach and scream some more."

I stuck my head out, my eyes still squinched shut, and yelled, "Help! Help!" as loudly as I could. The soldiers must have heard me, because I opened my eyes to see them galloping toward us, shouting and shooting, Mr. Cody leading them. One by one, the Indians fell off their ponies onto the ground. I didn't know whether to be horrified or relieved. I thought they had all been killed until I saw they were smiling. The soldiers got off their horses and, sweeping off their hats, bowed to the cheering audience. I couldn't believe my eyes. The Indians were springing up from the ground and bowing. The audience was stamping its feet and screeching with excitement. One woman in the audience fainted. It was Mama.

CHAPTER FOUR

Mr. Nelson and a man named Buck Taylor helped Mama back to our tent. When she was inside, her feet gave out from under her, and she sank down on a chair.

"I'm just fine now," Mama said in a shaky voice. "You go along, and I thank you for your kindness." She tried to smile, but it was like putting on a shoe to hide a big hole in your stocking. The hole wouldn't go away. As soon as the men left, she gathered me into her arms. "Miranda," she moaned, "when I saw the Indians going after the stagecoach and heard you screaming, I thought the world was coming to an end. I believed the Indians were going to kill you like they killed your dear papa."

I was just about to tell her I had felt the same way when an Indian woman walked into our tent. Mama held me tighter and cried out. I didn't think the woman looked very dangerous. She was holding a baby in her arms, and a child of two or three was clutching at her skirt. Young Wolf, Quick Fox, and Small Snow pushed in beside her. Quick Fox said, "This is my ma, Two Sky."

Two Sky was a large woman, as big as a man, but soft. Her dress looked like it was stuffed with pillows, only it was all her. You could hardly see the baby, for it was snuggled in all the softness. Two Sky wore fringed buckskin leggings and a buckskin shift whose yoke was fashioned of bright blue beads. Her hair hung in two untidy braids that were tied with frayed ribbons. Her smile was kind but weary, as if it didn't have much hope. Mama looked like she was trying to get words together to tell her to go away, but Two Sky took charge.

"Quick Fox," she ordered, "take the baby and Bear Paw back to our tepee."

Quick Fox gathered up the baby and took the toddler by the hand, and all five children disappeared. "Mr. Nelson said to me, 'Come, take care of the lady.'" Mama backed away and sat down, bewildered, on her cot.

Two Sky dipped a cloth into the washbasin and, after wringing it out, laid it gently on Mama's forehead. A little of the fear went out of Mama's eyes.

"The stagecoach is all show," Two Sky said. "Nothing to worry about. Why are you afraid of me? When I came into the tent, you looked like I came to chop you up. My husband is a good Indian. He was a scout with Mr. Cody in the Fifth Cavalry."

Mama looked embarrassed. Two Sky had come to help. "Please sit down, Two Sky." I knew those words were hard for Mama to get out.

Two Sky sat cross-legged on the blue rug. "I know your husband was killed with Custer. It was a time of war. Custer came to kill my people. We killed him instead. Then your people chased our people off our land and up to the Grandmother's country. Now we have come back, so who knows what will happen? Men want to be warriors." There was that tired look again, like the look of a rabbit that has been chased too long.

I was startled to hear such a speech. No one had ever dared say such things against Custer in front of us. I sneaked a look at Mama. Her eyes were very large in her pale face. I knew that angry words were coming, but at that moment Two Sky noticed the window Mama had painted on the tent's canvas. She threw her arms up in the air in surprise and hurried to examine it, nearly toppling the furniture in her path. "You make a sky. You make trees. You make birds." She laughed. "I'll tell my people. Now our land is all gone, you can show us how to make new land." She turned to me. "I will go now. You take care of your ma. When she feels good, you come and see the children again. See how we live in our tepee, snug like a nest of squirrels."

After Two Sky left, Mama breathed a sigh of relief. "In spite of such slander against General Custer I'm sure that woman meant well," she said, "but she's still one of them." Suddenly her face took on a startled look. "She said for you to come and see the children again." Mama gave me a sharp look. "Then those three Indian children must be the children Mr. Cody spoke of. You spent the afternoon with *them*?"

"Yes, Mama," I said slowly. "They're really nice. They took me to the parade and into the stagecoach." As I talked, I realized I was telling the truth. The Indian children *were* nice. "The older girl is Quick Fox, the little girl is Small Snow, and the boy is Young Wolf."

Mama wasn't listening. "I don't want you seeing them again, or you'll surely pick up their wild ways."

I didn't say anything, but inside I knew I wanted to see them again, even if it meant disobeying Mama. I had never had such an exciting day. To cover up my thoughts, I asked, "Mama, what is the 'Grandmother's country' Two Sky talked about?"

"That's Canada. The 'Grandmother' is Queen Victoria. It's a pity that Sitting Bull and his tribe ever left that land."

≈ ≈

The next day Mama was back at work on the Wyoming backdrop. Having a paintbrush in her hand always makes her happy. I sat quietly in the big tent watching her for a while, and when I saw a smile on her face, I dared to ask, "Mama, can I go and see the tepee? Two Sky invited me."

Mama looked up from her work, and the smile was gone. "No, Miranda. What would your papa think of your mixing with Indians?"

"There were Indians who fought *with* Papa," I pointed out. It was true. The Crows were scouts for Papa's regiment, and some of them died with Custer at the Battle of the Little Big Horn.

"Don't answer back, Miranda. Anyhow, that's quite different. The Crows were friendly to us. It was Sitting Bull's Sioux who killed Papa, and Two Sky is a Sioux. So are her children."

It wasn't fair. There were so few children at Fort Lincoln that I had never really had any friends. I liked Quick Fox and Small Snow and Young Wolf. I didn't see why I couldn't visit them. For the first time, I began to wonder if Mama might be wrong about Indians—at least some of them. Then I thought of Papa, and I was ashamed of myself.

Mama went back to work on her painting, and I wandered over to where the horses were kept. The stable made me think of Fort Lincoln and Comanche. There must have been fifty or sixty horses lined up in their stalls. I recognized the different kinds from the horses at the fort. There were heavy work horses, Clydesdales and Percherons; sassy mustangs; palominos with their elegant pale-blond manes and tails; and black Arabians looking like storybook horses.

The animal pens were near the stables. You could smell them long before you got there. The pens were like a Noah's ark. There were pairs of elk with their white bottoms, and shy deer and slim-ankled antelope. There were coyotes with narrow slanted eyes and bushy tails, and even a mountain lion with green eyes and a snaky tail. The mountain lion sat sulking in its pen like a child who has been locked in his room for punishment. Best of all were the buffalo with their curved horns, tiny eyes, shaggy coats, and dainty feet. Their shoulders were hunched and their heads were bent. They looked stubborn. They looked so much like great blocks of wood, I was surprised when they moved. I wondered if the animals crowded into that small space dreamed of the great forests and prairies where they had once lived.

Mr. Racher was pitching hay into their pens. "Hello there, little lady," he called out.

"Mr. Racher, don't you think the animals would be happier if they were free?" I asked.

"I know what you mean, Miranda, but think of it this way. If they were in the wild, something might get them. There's no animal but what some other animal out there wants to eat it up, including man. Anyhow, one day this will be the only way to see them. The buffalo are going fast. They get killed for meat. They get killed for their skin. They even get killed because there are people in the big towns who like to eat buffalo tongues."

Horrified, I asked, "Is anyone going to kill these buffalo?" I thought of coming in the dark of night and opening their pens, but then I wondered how they would escape through the streets of Chicago.

"No, indeed, little lady. Mr. Cody thinks as much of them as Annie does that poodle of hers."

"What's a poodle, Mr. Racher?"

"Well, I'd call it half a dog and half a toy," he said, chuckling.

On the way back I peeked into Annie Oakley's tent. There, on a cushion, was a poodle dog, white and curly as a lamb. And there was Annie Oakley, looking much smaller and younger than she did in the show. She grinned at me. "I know who you are," she said. "Your mama is painting the backdrops for us. She must be one talented lady. Come on inside."

I couldn't believe I was being invited into the famous Annie Oakley's tent. I guess I was standing there with my mouth open, because she said, "Come on, girl, no one's going to bite you."

The tent was much larger than ours and much more fancy. It looked like something out of *The Arabian Nights*. It was a perfect place for someone as amazing as Annie Oakley. There was a red vase with green-and-blue peacock feathers. Draped over a footstool was a tiger skin. The floor was covered with brightly colored rugs. On the chairs and bed were wondrously embroidered pillows.

She saw me admiring them. "I do the embroidering while I'm sitting around between shows."

Even though I knew it was rude, I couldn't stop staring at Annie Oakley. I thought she was the most incredible person I had ever seen. It didn't seem possible that the same person who could do just about anything in the world with a gun could hold a tiny needle and do such delicate stitching. I apologized for peeking into her tent. "I heard you had a poodle, mam, and I've never seen one."

She picked the white curly bundle up in her arms. "His name is George," she said. "And you can call me Annie. What's your name?"

"It's Miranda, mam." I was too shy to call her Annie.

"Would you like to hold him, Miranda?" she asked.

I nodded and stretched out my arms. The poodle with his soft warmness just fit into them. After a bit I handed him back. There were a thousand things I wanted to ask her, but all I could manage to say was "Thank, you, mam."

"Come and have a talk sometime," Annie Oakley said.

After I left Annie's tent, I felt like I was walking on clouds. As I wandered over to the big tent where Mama was working, I couldn't stop thinking about how different Annie was from Mama. Annie was more plainspoken. I thought I would be able to talk with her about almost anything.

In the tent several people were watching Mama working on the backdrop. It was huge: twenty feet long and fifteen feet high. They had even made a kind of scaffold for Mama so she could reach the top when she needed to. Mama had only been working on the backdrop for two days, but already she had finished painting a whole mountain. It would make me nervous to be watched, but Mama goes right into the world she is making. She doesn't know anyone else is there. When Mr. Cody came into the tent, swept off his hat, and greeted her, she jumped in surprise.

"I didn't mean to give you a scare, mam, but you've worked a miracle with that backdrop. You are truly an artist. I have been so lonesome for Wyoming, it does me good just to look at your painting. That snow on the mountaintop is so real, I could scoop it up. You truly have a gift."

Mama flushed with pleasure. "Never having seen Wyoming, I've had to copy the pictures you gave me. I couldn't tell if I was getting it right. I'll wait to put the animals in until I have time to make some sketches of them. I've seen the pens."

"When you're ready, I'll get someone to escort you there, and they can bring the animals as close as you like."

"Oh, not too close," Mama said hastily. "Just how is this canvas to be used?"

"It will serve as a backdrop for our acts. You see, mam, most people can't travel to the Wild West. They will never see what has been life and breath to me. I vowed I would bring the West to them. I have the Indians and the cowboys, and the animals. Until now I haven't had the look of it."

Mr. Cody noticed me. "Well, young lady, when I saw you stick your head out of that coach yesterday and scream, I said, 'There is a natural-born actress.'" He turned to Mama. "I only regret her acting was so good it frightened you, mam. You understand now that no harm was meant. With your permission I would like to put Miranda right in the show. If you can work up a scream like that every day, young lady, I'll pay you fifty cents a show. What do you say to that?"

"Oh, yes, sir!" I answered. I didn't tell him that I had screamed because I couldn't help it. Now I would be an actress, a part of the show. Scared as I had been inside the stagecoach, I remembered what it was like in the center of the ring with everyone looking at us and cheering. It was the first time in my whole life I had felt important.

When I looked up, I saw that Mama's lips were all ready to say no, but with a tip of his hat, Mr. Cody was gone. "Oh, Mama, please," I begged. I could see that the no was still coming, and I was desperate. At Fort Lincoln my life had been very small. Now it was getting bigger. I had been in Annie Oakley's tent, made friends with Indians, and ridden in a stage-coach that had been robbed by real outlaws. I didn't know what was coming next, but I wanted to find out. I didn't want to stop its happening.

"Mama," I pleaded, "it's just a show, and it only

takes a few minutes." Mama was shaking her head. I had to think of something. Quickly, I worked out the arithmetic. "Mama, even if we only do ten shows a week—that could be nearly a hundred dollars for the season!" After I said the amount, I could hardly believe how huge it sounded. I knew Mama was adding up what it could mean for the farm. She sighed and went back to her painting. That meant yes. I had gotten Mama to agree!

Mama began to paint a pine tree. It grew green and tall. At the top she put an eagle. "Put one in the air, Mama." And she did. Its great black wings stretched out as it rode the air currents. Nothing could hold it back. I felt like I was the eagle, flying higher and higher.

When I saw Mama was lost in her painting again, I took off at a run for the Indian village, even though I knew she wouldn't approve. I had to tell Quick Fox that I was going to be in the show with her. When I reached the village, I was a little afraid and hung back at first. But soon I found myself searching for Quick Fox's tepee. Some of the tepees were made of canvas, but many were covered with birch bark or woven mats. Kettles were slung over fires. Indians, some still in the war paint and feathers they wore in the show, were sitting at the entrances to their tepees, talking with one another. Visitors to the show were strolling through the village, curious to see how the Indians lived. They looked into the kettles and peeped into the tepees.

When I had found her, I asked Quick Fox, "Doesn't it bother you to have people staring at you?"

She only laughed. "They look at us, we look at them. They pay to look at us. We look at them for free."

Young Wolf shrugged. "If we were on our own land, they wouldn't dare poke their noses into our business."

"When will we ever be on our own land?" Quick Fox asked with a sigh. She gave me a little nudge. "Come in, Miranda. You will see what's in our tepee."

Cautiously, I went inside, not knowing what to expect. I was surprised at how neat and pretty it was, with six cots all covered with brightly colored blankets.

"I'll show you what my daddy bought me," she said, and began hunting around in a trunk. She handed me a pair of earrings with blue stones speckled with brown like a robin's eggs. "They're turquoise," she said. "That's a precious stone. You want to try how they look on you?"

Mama had never let me wear earrings. She said I was too young to have my ears pierced. I held them to my ears and looked into a hand mirror Quick Fox held up for me.

"My ma could fix your ears so you could wear them," she said. "I'd let you borrow them anytime you want."

I shook my head. "I don't think my mama would let me." Suddenly I remembered why I had come. "But she said I could ride the stagecoach in the show."

Quick Fox asked, "How come she's letting you?"

Feeling important, I said, "I changed her mind."

"She said yes even if we're in the coach with you?"

I blushed and stammered, "Sh-she doesn't care about that."

Quick Fox saw my embarrassment. "Your ma doesn't like us because we're Indian."

The truth just came out. "It's because of my papa getting killed by Sitting Bull's people."

Quick Fox gave me a sharp look. "If she doesn't

like Sitting Bull, she's going to be in trouble."

"What do you mean?"

"Sitting Bull is going to be part of the show."

"I don't believe you."

"I don't care. There's plenty you don't know. Sitting Bull is what Mr. Cody calls a big drawing card. A lot of people will come to see him because he's a famous warrior."

I started to say that Sitting Bull was an evil man, but just then Young Wolf and Small Snow came running up.

Young Wolf said, "We heard from Mr. Cody that you're going to be in the show."

"He said you had the best scream he ever heard." Small Snow laughed.

My argument with Quick Fox over Sitting Bull was forgotten. For the rest of the afternoon we practiced my scream, much to the alarm of the visitors. It was only when I started back to our tent that I remembered about Sitting Bull. I didn't know what Mama would say when she heard about the chief joining the show. I decided not to tell her, because I was afraid she might want to go home. Then there would never be enough money for us to live on the farm.

CHAPTER FIVE

The days flew by. Each afternoon, when the show was over and the people climbed into their wagons and carriages or boarded the streetcars to go home, I got to stay. For me the show was never over. Now that Mama had said I might be in the show with her, Quick Fox and I went everywhere together, and Small Snow trailed happily along. Quick Fox was full of gossip about the show. While I was still shy with the performers, she wandered in and out among the tents, chattering away to the Mexican riders and the cowboys, the cavalry soldiers and the work crews.

The whole show, even the animals, traveled from city to city by railway. It seemed impossible that the acres of tents and all the people and animals would fit into railway cars. "It's like a miracle," I told Quick Fox as we watched the men loading and unloading the railway cars, setting up the tents when we came to a town and striking them when it was time to move on.

The biggest tent was the mess tent, where everyone in the show had their meals. Mama was particular about what she and I ate. When we had first joined the show, she had fixed our meals in our tent. "There is talk a rat climbed into one of the kettles," she told me. "It got boiled with the stew. And that's not all. With Indians in the show you might find a dog cooked up for supper." But cooking in our tent turned out to be too much trouble. After a week Mama gave up and said we would eat with the others.

I liked being with the other members of the show and hearing their stories. Food was served family style, with people sitting on long benches. Heaping platters of chicken and bowls of stew were passed up and down the tables. There were great mountains of potatoes and steaming heaps of corn. Mama was a little shy at first, but soon she was talking with the work crew and the cowboys and Annie. It was hard to be standoffish while you reached for a pork chop or a piece of apple pie.

Quick Fox and I often sneaked into the wardrobe tent where costumes were kept. We loved to try on the clothes. I pranced around in the sombreros of the Mexican riders. Quick Fox clumped about in cowboy boots and a cowboy hat halfway down her face. One afternoon we put on the feather headdresses of the Sioux chiefs with eagle feathers that went right down to the ground. As we paraded back and forth in front of a tall mirror, Quick Fox said, "You'd make a good Indian."

Through the tent flap I saw Mama in the distance on her way back to our tent. She couldn't see me, but suddenly I felt funny in the headdress.

Quick Fox was watching me as I hastily removed my headdress. "Have you told your ma about Sitting Bull yet?" she asked.

I shook my head.

"What will she do when she finds out?"

"I'm afraid she'll want us to leave."

"Do you want to?" Quick Fox asked.

"No. I love it here. There's so much to do." I looked at her. "And I've got friends now."

She grinned at me. "I'm glad you joined the show." We didn't talk about being friends anymore. We just knew we were.

The show had a regular routine. The animals were watered and fed each day. Annie Oakley practiced her shooting. Sometimes she and Mr. Cody or their friend Set Glover would have a contest shooting at nickels or half-dollars. Annie always won. One morning Quick Fox and I watched a Mexican cowboy, Joe Esquivel, challenge the Indians to a horse race, and the whole camp was covered with clouds of dust. Another day Mr. Cody showed us how he could ride his horse with a full cup of water sitting on top of his head. He didn't spill a drop!

My favorite thing was to watch Mr. Cody using sign language to talk with the Indians. His hands and the Indians' moved like fluttering birds' wings as their conversation went back and forth without a sound. Quick Fox knew a few phrases in sign language, which I got her to teach me. When I tried to show Mama, she said, "Miranda, what have those Indian children been teaching you? You don't have to do tricks like that when you can talk perfectly well."

Mama's feelings about the Indians hadn't changed. That started me worrying all over again that she would want to leave the show when she heard that Sitting Bull would be joining it.

At the end of May Mama's backdrop of Wyoming

went up for the first time. The people in the audience cheered and clapped their hands. Seeing the mountains and trees and waterfalls stretched out in front of them was like traveling two thousand miles in a minute. Mama was standing next to me. Her face was flushed with pleasure at their applause. Yet she was not satisfied with her work. "I only wish I had more than pictures in a book to copy," Mama said. "There's not enough heart in the work."

This time Mama stayed beside me to watch the show, crying out in excitement when the cowboys rode standing up, one cowboy astride two and then three and finally four horses. She even stayed for the attack on the stagecoach. Afterward Mama said, "When the Indians went after you, and I heard you scream, I had to cover my eyes." But there was no fainting this time.

Together we watched the buffalo hunt. The buffalo were prodded into the center of the park. They milled around, their heavy heads swinging from side to side. Mr. Cody and the cowboys came riding in shouting. They aimed their rifles at the buffalo and shot. They didn't use real bullets, but the noise and smoke from the guns panicked the animals. They began galloping this way and that. There was more shooting, and then the buffalo were driven away. This was my least favorite part of the show. With actors everyone knew they were pretending. But the buffalo didn't know. They hadn't been able to say yes or no to being in the show.

Buck Taylor and Con Groner and the other cowboys roped steers, grabbing them by their horns and forcing them down to the ground, where they rolled their eyes and grunted. Seth Hathaway came racing in on his horse. Without slowing down, he and another rider exchanged mailbags to show how the Pony Express used to work. Mama clapped as hard as anyone. Now, I thought, Mama is enjoying the show, Indians and all. But I knew these Indians were one thing; Sitting Bull was another.

༄

It was early in June, and we had been with the show for over a month, when one day Mr. Cody stuck his head through the flap of our tent. "Mrs. James, mam, I wonder if I could have a word with you. Miranda, how are you on this fine day?" Though he was as affable as ever, I noticed creases from a frown upon his forehead and a nervousness in his hands.

Just as when he used sign language with the Indians, his hands seemed to be sending a message.

"Won't you sit down, Mr. Cody?" Mama asked.

"Thank you, mam, but I have to make arrangements for our opening in Buffalo tomorrow. That's why I came to see you."

Mama looked troubled. "I hope with the backdrop done you still have need of me?"

Mr. Cody quickly reassured her. "Yes, indeed, I certainly have need of you. There are posters to do, and then we will surely need a second backdrop with a scene of Montana and perhaps one of the Little Big Horn River." Mama's back stiffened. Hastily, Mr. Cody said, "I beg your pardon, mam. I know your dear husband was killed at the Battle of the Little Big Horn. The name of that river must bring back sad thoughts. That's why I'm here. I stopped by because I wanted to be the one to tell you myself. In the event you might be a little put out, seeing as how you feel about him."

"About who, Mr. Cody?"

"Sitting Bull, the Sioux chief."

I held my breath and stole a look at Mama. Suddenly I was ashamed that I had known about

Sitting Bull all this time and hadn't told her. Mama had turned beet red at the sound of Sitting Bull's name.

"Well, there is no puzzle there, Mr. Cody. If I saw the man who was responsible for the murder of my husband and his comrades, I would choke that man with my bare hands and trample him to death."

Mr. Cody bit back a smile, for Mama is slim as a flower stem. "I hope you don't mean that, Mrs. James, for Sitting Bull is joining the show when we open in Buffalo."

In a voice full of anger Mama said, "How could you allow such a thing?"

"Well, mam, I have to tell you I've known Sitting Bull a long time. I've fought against him, and I can honestly say he's a brave warrior and the Sioux's greatest chief. He deserves to ride at the head of the parade."

"What can you be thinking, Mr. Cody?" Mama cried. "Bringing Sitting Bull here is surely an insult to the memory of General Custer and his men. Men like my husband died at the hands of Sitting Bull and his warriors."

"I have great admiration for General Custer,

Mrs. James. I served as a scout for him back in '68. But he was always a man who did what he pleased. I don't like to say it, but it was Custer who started the Battle of the Little Big Horn. And it was Custer who disobeyed orders and led his men against Sitting Bull."

Mama's face was all puffed up. "I won't hear anyone say General Custer was not a brave man. He was a hero in the Civil War. That is the man your Sitting Bull killed."

I put my arm around Mama. She was right to stand up for Papa and the Seventh Cavalry. I wished Mr. Cody wouldn't put Sitting Bull into the show. But I didn't want Mama to be so angry we would have to go back to Dakota.

"I don't say he's 'my' Sitting Bull," Mr. Cody said. "You forget, mam, I fought with the soldiers at War Bonnet Creek to avenge Custer's death. I understand how you feel about your husband, Mrs. James, but the war is over. There is much to admire in Sitting Bull. When we get to Buffalo, Sitting Bull will ride at the head of the parade." Mr. Cody made a little bow to Mama and left.

Mama threw her arms around me and nearly

smothered me. "I would die of starvation rather than be in the same show with that horrible man," she sobbed. I clung to Mama. I was afraid she would say we had to go back to Fort Lincoln; at the same time I wasn't sure I wanted to stay in the show with Sitting Bull. There was something else about Mr. Cody's speech that bothered me. Why was he defending Sitting Bull? He had almost said that what Sitting Bull did was right. Everything was all tangled up, and I couldn't find my way out of the puzzle.

That night Mama tossed and turned in her camp bed. At last she sat up and lit our lantern. "Miranda, why would Mr. Cody make some sort of hero of Sitting Bull? How can he think we would stay any-where near that evil man?" She took up Papa's por-trait. "How can I look at your papa's face and stay in this show?"

"We don't have to have anything to do with Sitting Bull, Mama."

"Indeed we don't!" Her voice was as cold as a Dakota winter.

Mama reached into her trunk and took out four weeks' worth of money. We had been saving nearly every penny since May, when we joined the show.

"Why are you counting our money, Mama?" I guessed, but I hoped I was wrong.

"I want to see how much we would have left after our train fare home."

"We've only been here a few weeks. You watched the show with me today and liked it a lot. And your backdrop, Mama, remember how everyone clapped when they saw it. Mr. Cody wants you to do another one."

"That's enough, Miranda. It's the middle of the night. You go to sleep."

I didn't sleep. I was trying to get used to the idea of being in the same show with Sitting Bull. Mama and everyone at Fort Lincoln hated him. I had been taught to see him as if he were the devil with horns and hooves, but probably he only looked like the other Sioux warriors in the show. Though it might be disloyal to Papa, I didn't want to leave. I thought of the excitement of careening across the park in the Deadwood coach, my head sticking out of the window, screaming. I thought of the Indian warriors smiling at me when the audience couldn't see them. I remembered how a boy in the audience had asked me, "Do you get to see the show every day?" When I said, "Twice a day," he couldn't believe my luck.

I thought about all the things I would miss about the show. Most of all I thought of our farmhouse with the cottonwood tree and the lilac bush and my own room waiting for me. If we left the show, we would never save enough money to live there.

Mama had thought about the farm, too. In the morning she announced that when the show traveled to Buffalo, we would go along. "I am determined to save enough money to work the farm, Miranda," Mama said. "I won't allow Sitting Bull to keep me from it, but you are not to so much as look at that evil man."

For my dear papa's sake I resolved to obey Mama. Still, when the time came for the parade through Buffalo that opened the show, I weakened. Mama was busy working on a new poster. Small Snow, Young Wolf, and Quick Fox coaxed me to go with them to the parade.

"Our chief will be there," Young Wolf said proudly.

I agreed to go, but I told myself I would shut my eyes when Sitting Bull rode by.

As always, Small Snow lagged behind. Anything could catch her eye, a string of ants or a pretty flower.

Quick Fox was telling me the latest news. "There was a fight between the cook and Buck Taylor. Buck said the cook threw the cow in the kettle without skinning him first."

"I've already seen Sitting Bull," Young Wolf interrupted. "The chief let me hold his shield. It has sacred power and protects him in battle." Young Wolf's walk had become a swagger. Since he had heard Sitting Bull was joining the show, he had been practicing riding the Indian ponies. "One day I'm going to be a warrior like our chief," he said, "and get back all the Indian land the white man stole." His voice was angry.

I thought of the arrowhead I had found in the creek on our farm. I wondered if my grandfather had been one of the white men who had stolen Indian land. What if Young Wolf and some warriors came one day and wanted our land returned to them? Would I give it back? I wasn't the one who had taken it, I reasoned.

Quick Fox said, "I just wish we could get back enough land so we wouldn't have to live on the reservation anymore."

"What's a reservation?" I asked.

"The government takes our land away and makes us move onto a reservation," Young Wolf explained. "At the reservation there's a government agency that gives us money every month in exchange for the land, but only if we Indians stay right there where the government can keep an eye on us."

"They made us go to the school on the reservation, and the school won't let us talk Sioux," Quick Fox added. "The government wasn't even going to allow Mr. Cody to have Indians in his show because they would have to be away from their reservations, but Mr. Cody convinced the government that traveling around the country would be educational for the Indians."

I followed along behind Quick Fox, thinking I might share some of our farm with her so she wouldn't have to go back to a reservation. It didn't seem fair that Quick Fox had no place of her own.

When we reached Buffalo's main street, we had to push our way through the crowds. The whole town had turned out to see the parade. It was early June, but warm weather had already come. We stood under trees that were like great green umbrellas. In the front yards of the wooden houses, pink and red roses were blooming. Their fragrance was sweet upon the June breezes. The women were in summer dresses and the men in shirtsleeves. School was over in Buffalo, and children were everywhere calling to one another and pushing to get a better view.

Mr. Cody, very handsome in his fringed buckskin jacket and wide-brimmed Stetson hat, led off to the music of the cowboy band. Behind him rode Sitting Bull on a light-gray horse. At the sight of Sitting Bull a great cheer went up. There were also angry boos. One man called out, "There's the Injun that killed Custer."

I should have run off or at least looked the other way. But I couldn't. I watched the man I had been taught to hate and despise. What I saw was a well-built Indian no taller or shorter than most, with the low forehead and high cheekbones of his tribe. He wore a buckskin shirt and leggings. Beneath his headdress of eagle feathers two thick braids wrapped in some animal skin hung down nearly to his waist.

Then I noticed his eyes. They looked hard at everyone, as if he could see right into you. Eagle eyes. In his belt was an evil-looking knife. Here was the man who had led his warriors against Custer and Papa. I shuddered and looked away.

A minute later I was staring at him again, unable to keep my eyes off him. Sitting Bull paid no attention to the cheers or the boos. He sat up straight on his horse as he rode along the street. A leader. I could see he was a man who did not have to look back to know his followers were marching with him. I wondered how he felt about riding in a parade and having people staring at him.

There were many more cheers than boos for Sitting Bull. Young Wolf's cheers were the loudest. With his chief before him, Young Wolf had lost his stealthy, watchful look.

Suddenly, standing next to my new Indian friends, I was ashamed of disobeying Mama and betraying Papa's memory. I turned quickly away, telling myself this was the chief who had sent his warriors against General Custer and Papa and his comrades. I thought of Papa buried near the Little Big Horn, too far away for me to put flowers on his grave. Papa was dead and gone, and Sitting Bull was riding at the head of a parade with people cheering him.

I don't know how long I stood there lost in my thoughts, but when I looked up, the parade was ending. I wasn't anxious to get back to Mama. My mind was full of what I had just seen. To pass a little time,

I wandered by Annie Oakley's tent. When she saw me, she beckoned me inside. I gratefully settled down to watch her embroider a new shirt. She worked her needle in and out of the material, and a whole garden grew. It was like Mama's paintings. Flowers appeared with no seeds and no earth and no rain.

I admired her work so much, Annie stopped what she was doing to teach me the lazy daisy stitch and French knots. But I hadn't Annie's patience; my French knots kept turning into snarls. I put my poor efforts down and picked up Annie's poodle, who snuggled against me.

"Where did you learn to do needlework, Annie?" I asked.

"At the poor farm, Miranda," she answered. "Just like your daddy, my daddy died when I was a little girl, and Mama couldn't afford to keep me. The poor farm gave me out to a cruel farmer who worked me from sunup to sundown. I wasn't but your age; still, I milked the cows and fed the chickens and did the cooking and cleaning. When I was too tired to work, they beat me. When I couldn't stand it anymore, I ran back to the poor farm, and then Mama took me home. I started shooting squirrels and rabbits and deer and sold the meat. I paid off my mama's mortgage with my gun."

George was curled up on my lap, snoring softly. I ran my fingers gently through his soft curls so as not to wake him.

"Maybe I'll end up on a poor farm," I said.

"Whyever in the world do you say that, Miranda?" Annie asked in surprise.

"Mama talks of leaving the Wild West Show," I told her. It felt good to confide in someone. "Mama hates Sitting Bull. But if we left now, we wouldn't have enough money for our farm."

"I guess I understand your mama's feelings, given what happened to your pa, but I don't share them. Sitting Bull is a friend of mine."

"A friend!" I cried, not sure I had heard right. "Oh, Annie, how can that be?"

"I met Sitting Bull last year in Minnesota, Miranda," Annie explained, setting aside her embroidery. "He saw me shooting and he wanted to meet me. He said I was a better shot than any of his warriors. He adopted me into his tribe of the Hunkpapa Lakotas and gave me the name Watanya Cicilla; that means 'Little Sure Shot.'"

"Annie!" I could hardly get the words out. "You're a member of Sitting Bull's tribe!" I felt my heart racing. As I hastily stood up, tumbling George from my lap, I mumbled some excuse and ran outside, my mind all full of mixed-up thoughts. How could Annie Oakley be friends with Sitting Bull? How could Mr. Cody allow him in the show? It didn't seem fair to Papa and General Custer and all the soldiers who had been killed by Sitting Bull's warriors. And it seemed strange that I knew how I felt about Sitting Bull when he was far away, but now that he was right here, I wasn't so sure.

CHAPTER SIX

Much as I wished to show my hatred for Sitting Bull, I could not keep from watching him. He seemed more like a tired old man than the devil Mama thought him. He walked with a slight limp, and often I would see him shade his eyes with his hand. Quick Fox said the sun hurt his eyes. Sitting Bull spent much of his time in front of the entrance to his tepee, fanning himself with a red-tailed hawk's wing feather. He signed his autograph or let people take his picture in exchange for money. Mama said, "That Indian has no shame."

But I was not sure about that. I had heard Sitting Bull sent much of the money home to his two wives and eleven children. The rest he seemed to give away to the ragged newsboys and bootblacks who hung about, eager to see a real Indian chief. When I mentioned it to Mr. Cody, he said, "Sitting Bull can't understand how when the white man has so much, there are children who have so little. Among Sitting Bull's people it's shameful for a man to own more than the other members of his tribe."

As we traveled from town to town, all the performers in the Wild West Show became friendly with Sitting Bull. Only Mama and a few of the retired cavalry officers kept hating him. The rest of the people often gathered around him to hear stories of the battles he had fought. I stayed away from him, but once, when I was passing his tepee, he called out to me.

"Yellow Hair," he said. His voice was soft and sad-sounding, like the doves that called on Dakota mornings. I turned and ran quickly away from the Indian camp.

Young Wolf was spending much of his time with Sitting Bull. He was full of admiration for Tatanka Iyotanka, which was Sitting Bull's Indian name.

"He counted first coup when he was only fourteen," Young Wolf said. "Only a year older than I am."

"What does that mean?" I asked, in spite of my resolve not to talk about Sitting Bull.

"It means he got close enough to hit his enemy

with a coup stick, and he got a white feather to wear. When he was wounded for the first time, he got a red feather."

"How can you admire someone who is always fighting?" I demanded.

"He isn't always fighting. Only when someone tries to take his land away. How would you like it if someone came and stole that farm you're always talking about?" He gave me an angry look. "I dare you to go and ask Sitting Bull whether the battle of the Little Big Horn was his fault or Custer's fault. You're just afraid of hearing the truth."

I was tired of Young Wolf's praise of Sitting Bull. I didn't like his calling me a coward. If my father had been brave enough to go to war against Sitting Bull, I would be brave enough to tell Sitting Bull what I thought of him.

"All right," I said, "I will."

As soon as the words were out of my mouth, I regretted them. The thought of talking to Sitting Bull scared me to death. But Young Wolf was watching me, a sly smile on his face.

When I hung back, Young Wolf and Quick Fox grabbed my hands and led me to the chief's tepee.

Small Snow trailed along behind, gathering the few wildflowers that grew in the dusty park.

A man was taking Sitting Bull's picture. "He's busy," I said quickly, glad of an excuse. "We can come back later."

Quick Fox would not let me go. When the man left, Young Wolf ran up to the chief and pointed toward me. I longed to run away and hide. I told myself to think of Papa's bravery. Taking a deep breath, I marched up to Sitting Bull. I felt myself shaking with fright. He smiled at me in a friendly way. The smile made many deep creases in his brown skin, so he looked very old.

"Yellow Hair," he said to me, and then he spoke other words I could not understand.

Young Wolf began to translate the chief's words. "You are welcome here," he said.

I would not let him be pleasant to me. I shot out my words at him as if they were coming from a gun. "Your people killed my papa at the Battle of the Little Big Horn."

Young Wolf was shocked. He wouldn't translate my words. "You are insulting the chief of the Sioux," he said.

"But it's the truth," I insisted. I fought back tears of anger.

Sitting Bull spoke to Young Wolf. He must have insisted on knowing what I said. When Young Wolf told him, the chief, instead of raging or roaring or gnashing his teeth as I expected, just looked sad. He motioned for me to sit down next to him.

"He wants to tell you about the battle," Young Wolf said.

I would not sit down but stood stiffly as Sitting Bull talked through Young Wolf.

"I had a vision long before that battle took place." Sitting Bull had a faraway look in his eyes, as though the vision were still before him. "I saw soldiers riding toward our village. They were as many as the little grasshoppers that leap about in the summer fields. The soldiers and their horses were upside down, their hats falling off. In my vision these soldiers had no ears. The dream told me of the battle that was coming."

His words were frightening and made no sense to me. "I don't understand what your dream meant," I whispered.

Young Wolf continued to translate. "To me, Yellow

Hair, it was very plain. The white man has no ears to listen to the Indian." Sitting Bull paused, and his face grew soft. "On the morning of the battle I heard meadowlarks singing," he said. "They are a brave bird, the last to leave us when the wind and snow come."

Before I could stop myself I said, "We have meadowlarks on my farm." Sitting Bull nodded, and I made myself remember that he was my enemy. I closed my mouth so I wouldn't say any other words.

"Long Hair came to our Paha Sapa," Sitting Bull said. His face grew hard. Young Wolf explained that Long Hair was what the Indians called General Custer, and that Paha Sapa were the Black Hills. "For two moons Long Hair and his soldiers tramped over our sacred land. All the while in their minds they were giving our land away. They were giving it to farmers who would put up fences where we hunted. They were giving it to the railroad to lay down tracks that would bring more farmers. They were giving it to the miners who wished to break open our hills and tear gold out of their very heart. Because they fought on his side, Long Hair even allowed our enemy the Crows to take our land. How could we trust Long Hair?"

As he talked, I tried to tell myself it was only right that settlers should have land to farm and that the great railroad should bring the two ends of the country together. At the same time a small voice inside me kept saying that the land belonged to Sitting Bull and his people. They must have loved it as I loved my farm.

Sitting Bull noticed the confusion on my face, for he paused for a moment and gave me a thoughtful look. "We moved to the Elk River and then to the Little Big Horn. Still the white man came." There was that look again. "How could we stand by while our land was taken from us, while game was driven off so no food was left for our children? We rode against the men who made the railroad, and against the miners with their pickaxes, and against the farmers with their fences. We chased them from our land, and when they did not go, some of our braves killed them. Then Long Hair came back with his soldiers, and your father among them."

From the expression on Sitting Bull's face, I guessed at what he was saying even before Young Wolf translated his words. I didn't want to hear any more of those words. I did not want words that would eat away at the anger I had taken such good care to keep. I knew Sitting Bull was going to tell the story of the battle in which Papa was killed. I was afraid to listen.

"It was a June day like this one," Sitting Bull was saying, "with everything warm where the sun touches it. My two wives and my children were in the woods picking wild strawberries. Some of our people were fishing in the river for the quick trout. Others were gathering the tender green shoots of the cattail. Still others were tending to our herds."

I had pictured Papa and the cavalry riding over the fields and down the hill to the river a thousand times, but I had always pictured Sitting Bull and his people as fierce warriors, never as he was describing them now.

"Then came a shout from one of our women. She saw Long Hair and his soldiers, and with them our enemy the Crow. Quickly our men put on their war paint, but already bullets were finding their way into our tepees. Our elders began to sing death songs for our warriors. I myself did not even have time to put a feather in my hair. The soldiers were upon us. They turned their guns into one of our tepees. Many were killed. Among them my friend's two wives and three of his little ones." Sitting Bull's voice grew hard. "They say I killed Custer. I did not. He was a fool and rode to his own death, and your papa with him."

I put my hands over my ears and would listen to no more. Quick Fox tried to put her arm around me, but I shook her off. This was not the story I had heard over and over at Fort Lincoln. It was not just the Indian warriors riding against the soldiers and killing them. It was something else. I didn't want to believe Sitting Bull. He was saying bad things about Papa and the cavalry. I stumbled blindly toward our tent. When I found Mama, I threw my arms around her, sobbing out the story Sitting Bull had told. I wanted her to explain it all away.

Mama gently smoothed my hair and wiped my tears, but when I looked up, her face was like a storm the moment before the lightning and thunder come.

"We will not stay here," she said. "It's as though that terrible man were killing your papa and the soldiers all over again."

"But Mama," I sobbed, "the soldiers shot the wives and children of Sitting Bull's friend. How could they do such a thing? The women and children weren't warriors." I was seeing the terrible scene inside my head.

Mama hardly listened to me. Her face was set and her voice hard. "Did Sitting Bull tell you of the settlers' wives and children his warriors had killed?" Slowly I shook my head. "Of course he didn't. I'm going to take you away from that evil man, Miranda. I can't have you listening to such tales. It's like being at war again. We have enough saved for railway fare back and a little to take care of us until I find work."

Sitting Bull's story had rattled all my ideas until they were shaken apart. Still I knew I did not want to leave the show.

"We can't go now," I cried. "If we do, we won't have enough money to live on our farm." I took Mama's hand and tried to reason with her. "Mama, you said yourself, 'Why should Sitting Bull be allowed to chase us away?'" But Mama only shook her head. I saw that my arguments were not going to change her mind. I wished I had never told Mama about Sitting Bull.

"I don't care if it means we will never have the farm," Mama said firmly.

"But I'll promise never to go near Sitting Bull

again," I pleaded. "I'll forget what he told me."

"It's no use, Miranda. I will not stay here one more moment. I'm going to find Mr. Cody and tell him so." Before I could stop her, Mama rushed from the tent.

I saw what I had done by running to Mama for comfort. Not only would I have to leave the show and my friends, but I had made us lose the chance to live on the farm. If Mama went back to being a laundress, she would never get enough money.

And there was something more. Something tangled in my mind. Mama's words and Sitting Bull's words were snarled together like the knots I got when I tried my hand at embroidering. If we left the show now, I knew I would never untangle the knot and find the truth.

Desperately I tried to think of how to keep Mama from taking us away. I was sure that as long as she had the money to return to Dakota, that was what she would do. No pleading on my part would change her mind. Suddenly an idea snaked into my head. What if she didn't have the money?

My hands were shaking as I opened Mama's trunk. I found her money box under her stockings and vests. I knew where it was because at the end of each week I would give her my dollars to save and she would give me twenty-five cents to spend as I liked. I told myself I wasn't stealing the money. I wasn't going to spend it. I was just moving it. Hastily, I took the money box and hid it in the bottom of my trunk. The touching of it seemed to burn my hands. The moment I did it, I wished I hadn't, but it was too late. Mama came hurrying back. I began tidying the tent so that she should not see my face.

She was out of breath. "I couldn't find Mr. Cody, but we must make arrangements at once for passage on a train." Mama opened her trunk. "Thank heavens we have put something aside."

My heart sank as Mama began searching frantically through the trunk, tossing things out onto the floor. I wanted so much to speak, but all my words disappeared.

At last Mama turned to me, a puzzled look on her face. "It's not here, Miranda! I don't understand." After a moment she said, "Someone has taken it. I didn't think we were traveling with thieves. But who can it be? Who would guess where I keep the money?" A harshness came upon her face so that I scarcely recognized her. "It's those Indian children you play with. They are always in and out of the tent. I knew if you ran about with them, there would be trouble." She was on her feet and moving toward the tent flap. "I'll go to Two Sky at once. She must deal with them."

Horrified, I grabbed at her. "Oh, Mama, wait. I'm sure it wasn't them. They would never do such a thing."

"How do you know that? They are Indian children, after all."

"They're my friends!"

Mama hesitated for a moment. "What am I to think? No one else comes into our tent."

My words were stuck in my throat. In a whisper I said, "I know they didn't take the money."

For the first time Mama was really looking at me. She took hold of my shoulders with both of her hands and stared into my eyes. "Then who could have taken it?" she asked, but she already knew.

"It was me," I sobbed. "I took it. I don't want to leave the show. I want us to have enough money to move to our farm. You can put me in jail for it."

Mama dropped her hands from my shoulders and

looked at me like she didn't know me. Hastily, I dug the money box out of my trunk and held it out to her. My hands were shaking. We were both crying.

"Miranda, how could you have done such a wicked thing?" Mama asked, in a voice I had never heard before.

I could not tell her, for I was not sure myself. There was one thing I knew: Mama and I were standing on the opposite banks of a river, and neither one of us could cross over. I think if I could have talked with Mama about Sitting Bull and Papa without her getting so angry, I would never have done such a bad thing. But Mama would not hear such talk.

At that moment Mr. Cody walked into our tent. He could see both Mama and I had been crying. Quickly he said, "Forgive me, mam. I was told you were looking for me. I'll be in my tent. You just let me know if there's anything I can do to help you. Anything at all."

Mama wiped her eyes and straightened up. "Thank, you, Mr. Cody."

When he had left, I asked in a small voice, "Can we stay?"

Mama sank down on a chair and put her face in

her hands. At last she looked up. "I don't know, Miranda. I can't help feeling that you would never have done such a bad thing if we were still in Dakota. I think it was wrong of me to bring you here." Mama had a sad look on her face, as though I had gone someplace where she couldn't find me.

After that, Mama was very quiet and I was very miserable. I crept out of the tent and wandered off into the park where the show had been set up. A man was mowing the lawn. I could smell the freshly cut grass. It made me think of Dakota and how good the hayfields smelled when they were cut. I thought about the farm, but for the first time thinking about it didn't make me happy. I had spoiled everything.

I was sitting on a bench, staring at a robin who was pulling up a worm and thinking that was me, a worm, when Quick Fox dropped down next to me.

"I saw your ma," she said, "and she looked like she could sting worse than a hornet, so I went to find you."

"She's mad at me. I told her what Sitting Bull said, and she wants to leave the show." I turned my head away. I couldn't look at Quick Fox while I admitted what I had done. "I stole our money so we couldn't pay for our fare back to Dakota, and Mama found out."

Quick Fox stared at me, her brown pebble eyes wide open. "You did a really dumb thing. No wonder she's mad. I guess Young Wolf shouldn't have made you talk to Sitting Bull."

"Sitting Bull was just telling the truth. Only there's the truth he believes and the truth Mama believes. I'm not sure what to think."

"It's like that for me sometimes. Young Wolf says we're supposed to hate the white man because he took our land, but we're friends with you and Annie and Mr. Cody and a lot of white people."

I had never considered how Quick Fox felt about white people. At least I wasn't the only person in the world trying to figure things out.

"If you can still be friends with us after we've taken your land, why is Mama so hard-hearted about Indians?" I asked. "Why won't she listen to Sitting Bull's side?"

"It's not just your ma. There's plenty who don't want to hear the Indian side. Like your ma, some of them had bad things happen to them. But the Indians did too. My grandpa got killed in a battle between his tribe and some soldiers."

"Your grandpa!"

Quick Fox's face became sad. "It was the year before I was born. It was at Arrow Creek. Spotted Eagle and his people had two thousand lodges. Nearby were five hundred soldiers. Spotted Eagle didn't much want to ride against the soldiers, but there were some hotheaded warriors who did, and my grandpa was one of them. They went against the soldiers by night, and my grandpa got killed for it."

I had never guessed that Quick Fox had lost someone just like I had. I put my hand on her arm. "I'm sorry about your grandpa," I said. And I was.

"I'm sorry about your pa." After a minute Quick Fox stood up. "I heard they're bringing in a railroad car of new buffalo," she said. "Let's go see them unload."

I got off the bench and followed her. There was a buffalo calf not more than a few months old. We stood there watching it trot along with its mother, its dainty hooves hardly touching the ground. Just seeing the calf made me feel better.

≈⋙

That night Mama said nothing more about leaving the show. But I could tell she was thinking about it. After she believed I was asleep, she got out of bed and counted our money. I knew she was wondering how far it would stretch if we left the show. Then a letter came that decided things for Mama.

A friend from Fort Lincoln wrote to tell us that more troops were being withdrawn from the fort. It was possible that the fort itself might be closed. Mama heaved a great sigh. "We must remain with the show, Miranda. If we were to return, there would likely be no laundress work for me at the fort, and we don't have enough money saved to live on the farm."

The sadness in Mama's eyes when she looked at me pierced me more than any of Sitting Bull's arrows might have.

CHAPTER SEVEN

The sadness stayed in Mama's eyes to remind me every day of the wicked thing I had done. It was only when we reached Washington that her sadness was swept away by all the excitement. We put on our best clothes for our visit to see the nation's capital. Everyone went: Annie Oakley, the cowboys in their chaps and broad-brimmed hats, and the Indians wearing their best buckskins and feathered head-dresses. We were taken by carriages into town. I suppose we were an unusual sight, for everyone stopped to stare.

It was a late June day, with a steamy heat coming off the Potomac River. We were so excited by the sights of the capital that we didn't mind the hot winds and the hungry mosquitoes that followed us everywhere.

Washington was a city of trees: elms, oaks, and maples lined the streets. Broadest of all the streets was Pennsylvania Avenue, which swept from the White House all the way to the Capitol building. The Capitol sat on the crest of a hill, so from far away you could see its great white dome ringed around with pillars. They looked like candles on a frosted birthday cake. At the very top of the dome, like a decoration on the cake, was the golden statue of Freedom.

As soon as we were out of the carriages, Quick Fox, Young Wolf, Small Snow, and I climbed over anything that might be climbed over. When we reached the Washington Monument, which had only just opened a few months before, we clutched one another and, craning our necks, stared at the top of the monument, which seemed to rush right up to the clouds. After that we chased one another around the monument until we were out of breath.

Best of all the places we visited was the White House, where the president lives. After the British had set it afire in 1812, the blackened stone was painted white. The building shone in the sun.

Small Snow said, "It's big enough for our whole tribe and for our horses, too."

Mama couldn't stop looking at everything. She quickly took out her drawing pad and pencil. "Miranda, I'm going around to sketch the back of the White House. I'm told it's like a glade there, with the rolling lawn and trees and then the great white house and its porches. You had better come with me."

"Mama, let me wait for you here," I begged. "I don't want to miss anything." People were asking to see the cowboys' guns and lariats and examining the beaded moccasins and feathered bonnets of the Indians. Carriages were bringing what I was sure were very important people to the White House entrance, where two soldiers stood stiffly on duty. Anytime, I thought, President Grover Cleveland himself might appear.

Annie Oakley promised to look after me, so Mama said I might stay. She had been gone only a few minutes when we saw one of the carriages from the show rolling down Pennsylvania Avenue. As it drew nearer, we could see Mr. Cody and Sitting Bull. A great cheer went up as they were recognized. I supposed that Mr. Cody and Sitting Bull were there to see the White House, and that the carriage would stop where ours had.

Instead, their carriage pulled right up the driveway to the entrance of the White House. I was glad Mama was not there when Mr. Cody and Sitting Bull stepped out together. Mr. Cody had on his best buckskin jacket. Sitting Bull had a jacket embroidered with glass beads. His braids were tied with bands of fur.

"What is he doing here?" I asked Quick Fox.

"It's why he came with the show," she said.

"What do you mean?"

Young Wolf proudly answered, "Sitting Bull said he would travel with the show if Mr. Cody promised to take him to the great tepee in Washington so he could give President Cleveland a letter."

"What kind of a letter?"

Young Wolf drew himself up. "I saw it. I saw Sitting Bull's letter. It's on the stationery of the Wild West Show and it's addressed to 'My Great Father.' He tells the president how all of our tribe's sacred lands have been taken away by the government. He demands to have them back."

"Will the president give his lands back?" I asked.

Young Wolf shook his head sadly. "I don't think so, but still a chief has to speak out for his people."

In that moment, as I watched Sitting Bull enter the White House, I realized that I felt sorry for him. My hate had started to melt around the edges, like river ice when the March thaw comes.

❧

Because of Mama's wishes, I kept away from Sitting Bull as we traveled through New York State and Connecticut and then to Boston. But Mama said nothing when I ran off to play with Quick Fox and Young Wolf and Small Snow. There were even times when she would visit with Two Sky. I heard them talk about what a strange place a Wild West show was to raise children.

Sometimes I would think about my life at the fort and how lonely I had been there. Now there was always something new to see and do. The Indians were fond of table tennis, so there was always a game to watch. The Indians let me look on as they mixed their war paint for the show. I learned black was made from charcoal or lampblack and the white and red and yellow from colored clay mixed with buffalo fat. The Indian women were even more talented with embroidery than Annie Oakley. I watched them work with tiny glass beads and porcupine quills dyed different colors. The women softened the quills by holding them in their mouths as they worked. The quills and beads were embroidered onto dresses and shirts and moccasins. The quills were even turned into fringes.

Buck Taylor, who was six and a half feet tall without his boots on, taught us how to braid a rawhide lariat and how to do rope tricks with it. Young Wolf could keep a circle spinning with a lariat while Quick Fox and I jumped in and out of it. Buck was a gentle man, but he could throw a steer by its tail and tie it up with one hand behind him. Con Groner told us stories of the time when he was sheriff of the Platte and brought in half a hundred murderers. Mr. Nelson had guided Brigham Young to Utah in 1847. But the best stories were Mr. Cody's.

When Mr. Cody was just eleven years old, his father had said right out in public that he was against slavery. For those brave words he was knifed in the back by people who wanted slavery. "I was no more than a child," Mr. Cody said. "If I hadn't gone to work, my family would have starved. I got me a job as a scout for wagon trains, looking out for Indians on the warpath. When I was only fifteen, I started working for the Pony Express. Can you believe that once, when the man who was supposed to relieve me was nowhere around, I had to ride three hundred twenty miles? And I did it in just twenty-two hours!"

I was walking home, trying to imagine what it would feel like to ride so fast, when I saw Annie Oakley coming from our tent, a worried look on her face.

"Miranda," she said in a hushed voice, "you had better see to your mama; she's not well. I'm going to speak to Mr. Cody."

I flew to our tent, Quick Fox, Young Wolf, and Small Snow hurrying along behind me. Mama was lying down on her cot. Her face was flushed as though she had been bending over a hot stove. When I put my hand to her forehead, it felt burning hot.

"Miranda, I have such a headache." Mama gave me a frightened look. "If anything should happen to me, who would look after you?"

Quick Fox had been standing at the entrance to the tent. Now she disappeared.

I took Mama's hand and hung on to it. Papa was gone. If something happened to Mama, I would be an orphan, all alone in the world.

"Now I'm so cold," Mama said in a shaky voice. Quickly I covered her with her blanket and then, because Mama could not stop shivering even on that hot July day, I put my own blanket on her as well. Mama's teeth were chattering, and her body was shaking with chills.

"Get Annie, Miranda," Mama whispered. "Get Annie Oakley."

But Annie had gone to find Mr. Cody. I saw Quick Fox, pulling Two Sky after her. Not mindful of manners, I grabbed Two Sky's arm.

"It's Mama," I said. "She's very sick. First she's hot; then she's cold. Please, can you come?"

Two Sky hurried toward our tent. I think Mama was too sick to notice that it was Two Sky who was there. She just lay still, her moans soft as a turtle-dove's call. Two Sky ordered all of us to stay outside.

"Don't worry, Miranda," Quick Fox said, trying to comfort me. "I'm sure your ma will be all right."

I hardly heard her words. I had never felt so alone. I thought of Mr. Cody having to make his own way when he was just my age, and Annie sent to the cruel farmer.

After a very long time Two Sky came out of our tent calling out orders: "Quick Fox, go get fresh water. Young Wolf, bring blankets from our tent. Small Snow, go with your brother. Hurry now, children."

As soon as they were gone, Two Sky said, "Miranda, hear me. Your mother is very sick. I worry for her."

I stared at her, trying not to cry. Two Sky put her arm around me. "Do not be afraid. I have seen this illness before. I know who can help your mother. There is a *wicasa*, a medicine man, in the show. He is a brave warrior but he is also a healer. Wherever he travels, he carries with him roots and barks. I will ask him what he can do."

Hopeful, I asked, "Which one of the Indians is it?"

Two Sky hesitated. "It is Sitting Bull."

Sadly, I shook my head. "Mama will never take his medicine," I said. "She would think it was poison."

"Yes. She does not forgive him. That is another kind of poison." Two Sky was silent for a moment. "If you want me to talk with Sitting Bull, you will tell me." She waited.

There was no time to say more, for Mr. Cody arrived with Annie. After one look at Mama, he hurried off to fetch a doctor.

When he came, the doctor frightened me. He was an elderly, stoop-shouldered man, dressed all in black and carrying a black bag. He looked like the turkey vultures that sat hunchbacked in the cottonwood trees around the fort. After he looked at Mama, he came out of the tent and asked Mr. Cody, "Where has your show been playing?"

Mr. Cody began to list the cities. When he came to Washington, the doctor stopped him. "I believe Mrs. James has malarial fever. She most likely got it in Washington. The fever breeds in the town's swamps. I wish I could prescribe some medicine that would cure her, but there is nothing to be done except wait out the attack. The woman who is with her seems a good nurse. And you, young lady," he said, turning to me, "you must do all you can to help your mother."

It was not just the doctor's words and his black suit but the solemn sound of his voice that frightened me. I hurried into the tent. Mama had thrown off her blankets and was in the midst of a fever again. Two Sky was bathing her forehead with cool water. A moment later Mama's teeth were chattering, and she reached for the blankets.

For two long days and two long nights Mama was either burning or freezing. She didn't eat and could not move from her cot. The doctor returned, but he only shook his head. Two Sky brought her own cot into our tent and would not leave Mama. When she saw me crouched next to the entrance of the tent, she would tell me, "Go with Quick Fox; there is nothing you can do here."

I would go off with Quick Fox for a few minutes, but then I would creep back to the tent. I could not leave Mama. With Mama so sick, I got very little sleep at night. When I did sleep, I had terrible nightmares. I dreamed I returned to our farmhouse and Mama was there, but the house grew smaller and smaller around Mama until it was no larger than a coffin.

By the morning of the third day Mama's chills and fevers were worse. I knew Mama's life might depend on what I decided. I was sure she wouldn't want medicine from Sitting Bull, yet that medicine might save her life. Without Mama to tell me what to do, I had to do what I thought was right.

I motioned Two Sky out of the tent and begged her, "Two Sky, you have to help Mama. I'm afraid she's going to die. Please, could you ask Sitting Bull for his medicine? Mama doesn't have to know."

She put her arms around me. "Go back in to your ma. I will see the chief." She hurried off.

When she returned, she had a powder. "You mix

this in water. Give it to your ma when the sun comes up, in the middle of the day, and when the sun goes down. Sitting Bull says it is finely ground bark from south Mexico. The chief traded for it with Mexicans in the show."

That noon, trying to keep my hand from trembling, I handed Mama the medicine to drink. She must have thought the medicine came from the doctor, for she drank it right down, whispering only, "How bitter."

Two whole days went by, and there was no change. I was afraid I had done the wrong thing, but on the third day, Mama was a little better, and I started to breathe again. The day after, she was sitting up in bed and taking a bit of broth. She even told me my hair wanted washing and combing. When the doctor came, he said, "It's just as I predicted. These malarial fevers burn themselves out. I believe she'll be fine now. She only wants rest."

I looked at Two Sky, who was gathering up her things. She gave me a quick smile. "I will go back to my tent now. You will care for your ma."

All that day I kept looking at Mama and feeling happy. She was becoming herself again. She was too weak to get up, but she talked of how the furniture in the tent needed dusting and told me to put on a clean pinafore. By the end of the week she had begun work on a poster. The doctor had said the fever had burned itself out, but I believed it was Sitting Bull's medicine that had made her well. Whatever it was, by the time we left for Canada, I knew that I had Mama safely back again, and that I had made the right choice.

CHAPTER EIGHT

The show played in Canadian cities like Toronto and Ottawa, and in Montreal, where people spoke French and called out "ooorrah" for hurrah. But I liked best the small Canadian farm towns like Kingston and Hamilton. Their fields of wheat and corn growing tall and green in the July sun reminded me of Dakota. Mama had her strength back and was finishing a backdrop of Montana for Mr. Cody.

Each time I saw Sitting Bull, I wanted to thank him for making Mama better. At last I got up the courage to visit his tent with Young Wolf. Sitting Bull was wearing a blue linen shirt and black Mexican pantaloons. Around his neck was a red handkerchief. He was sitting cross-legged on a blanket combing his shiny black hair, which hung down to his waist. There was a mirror beside him.

"Young Wolf," I said, "please tell Sitting Bull I am grateful to him for helping Mama when she was sick."

Young Wolf translated Sitting Bull's answer: "I am glad your mother is well. I, too, am better, for I am happy to be in the Grandmother's land again." Sitting Bull carefully braided his hair.

"Why is that?" I asked.

"After the Battle of the Little Big Horn, the *akicita*, the soldiers, came to fight us." Young Wolf continued to translate, sometimes pausing to repeat a Lakota word before he spoke the English, as though the English were a poor substitute. "They hunted us down. They wanted to put us on a reservation. We escaped to the Grandmother's country, and they welcomed us."

"Then why didn't you stay here?" I asked.

Sitting Bull shrugged. "The *tatanka*, the buffalo, were disappearing in the Grandmother's country. Also, I wanted my children to grow up in their native land. How could I know that when I returned, I and my tribe would be prisoners at the Standing Rock reservation?"

Sitting Bull wrapped thin strips of otter skin around each braid as he talked. "At the reservation they took our ponies away and gave us cows." He laughed, but the laugh was a bitter one. "Who can ride a cow across the plains?" he asked. "The white men promised us the Black Hills would be ours as long as the grass grows and the rivers run. They did not keep their promise. My heart is in the Paha Sapa, the Black Hills." He shook his head. "I'll never see them again."

I understood how Sitting Bull felt. After all the time we had spent in cities, I was beginning to long for Dakota and my farm. Still, I knew that in the fall, when the show closed, the farm would be there. It was different for Sitting Bull. He would never be able to go back to his Black Hills.

All that day I thought about Sitting Bull. When I saw Quick Fox, I told her what he had said. "I wish I could find a way to let Sitting Bull return to the Black Hills."

She shook her head. "I don't see how. The government keeps an eye on him. He had to get special permission to come with the show, and he had to promise to go back to the reservation. They'd never let him go to the Black Hills."

I thought some more. "What if we brought the Black Hills to him?" I asked.

She looked at me like I was crazy. "What do you mean?"

When I told her, she grinned. "Sure," she said, "if you can talk your ma into it."

That afternoon I went to see Mr. Cody. As usual, his tent was crowded with cowboys, for he dearly loved to exchange stories with them. Buck Taylor was squeezed into a chair, his long legs sticking out like two stovepipes. Doc Middleton was there, and Con Groner. Con was telling a story about when he was a sheriff and kept Jessie James's gang from holding up a Union Pacific train east of North Platte. "You had to work plenty fast to keep ahead of James," he said.

"Well, I guess you were the man for that," Doc Middleton said. "You sure kept coming after me."

Doc had been a real bandit in Nebraska when Con had been sheriff. Now they were both in the show, and after years of shooting at each other they were friends. I thought that was a little like Sitting Bull and me.

At last Con and Doc and Buck Taylor wandered out of the tent. I sat there wondering how to begin. I guess Mr. Cody could see I was anxious to talk to him, because he said, "Well, Miranda, it looks like you've got something on your mind. You go right ahead and tell me what it is."

Suddenly my idea seemed a foolish one, but I could see Mr. Cody was waiting for me to speak up. I took a deep breath. "Mama's finished the backdrop of Montana and the posters, Mr. Cody. Do you think you could you ask her to do a backdrop of the Black Hills?"

"Well, I hadn't thought of it, but that would do just fine as a backdrop for your Deadwood coach. The coach came from the mining town of Deadwood in the Black Hills. What a lot of hearts were broken at that place! The cemetery there is full of desperate men who put bullets through their heads when they didn't find gold." He patted my hand. "But you didn't come to hear me talk. Tell me, Miranda, what put the idea into your head of a backdrop of the Black Hills?"

Hastily I blurted out, "It's for Sitting Bull. He misses the Black Hills, and he knows he'll never get them back."

"Why are you so interested in Sitting Bull all of a sudden? I thought, like your mama, you didn't care much for him."

"I know how he feels about the Black Hills," I answered. "It's how I feel about my farm."

Mr. Cody pushed back his Stetson and gave me a long look. "It's more than that, Miranda, isn't it?"

I nodded. "When Mama was sick, Sitting Bull gave her some medicine. Only I didn't tell her it was from Sitting Bull or she wouldn't have taken it. It doesn't seem right that she should dislike him so much after he made her well."

Mr. Cody smiled. "So that's it. Is your mama still ready to choke him with her bare hands and then trample him to death?"

"Yes, sir, but I don't think she would hate him so much if she got to know him."

"Is that what happened to you, Miranda?"

"Yes, sir. Young Wolf made me talk to Sitting Bull. I got to know what happened at the Battle of the Little Big Horn. After that I began to feel different about Sitting Bull, only it's taken me a long time to admit it."

Mr. Cody had been watching me closely as I talked. "Well, young lady," he said, "I'll stop by and have a talk with your mama after lunch."

"If she knew the idea came from me, she might

think Sitting Bull or Quick Fox put me up to it. You won't tell her I suggested it?"

"I swear I won't say a word." Mr. Cody reached out and patted my hand. I felt better, but I still worried that I was being disloyal to Mama and Papa. I had gone behind Mama's back to get her the medicine, and now I was tricking her into doing something for Sitting Bull. I hoped Mama would change as I had. Maybe not so much, but at least a little. I wanted some of the hate and bitterness over Papa's death to go away so she could be happy again.

Mama was always glad to see Mr. Cody, pronouncing him a "real gentleman." When he poked his head with his big Stetson hat through the tent flap later that afternoon, Mama welcomed him. "Come in, sir. We're very pleased to see you."

In a polite gesture he swept off his hat, a rare thing. Quick Fox had told me he slept in it. "I have a request to make of you, mam. What would you think of doing a backdrop of the Black Hills?"

I gave Mama a nervous look, but her face had taken on a shine. "Why, that's a wonderful idea. My other work is just about finished and I want to earn my keep. Of course, I've never seen the Black Hills, but I suppose you have some pictures you could show me?"

"I have something better than pictures. I have a man who knows the Black Hills as well as anyone in the world. He can tell you every bird and animal and tree. More important, he will tell you all of this from his heart, for those hills were his home, and they mean everything to him."

Mama was excited. "Nothing could suit me better, Mr. Cody. To be truthful, it's what I think is missing in the Montana backdrop. I only had pictures and my imagination. I would welcome working with someone who knows the country well and has a love for it. Is it one of the cavalry officers or one of the cowboys?"

"It is an Indian, mam."

I saw a shadow steal across Mama's face. She held herself more stiffly. "I don't say I would choose to work with an Indian, but if he can help me to make a finer painting, then I will be willing to do it."

I held my breath. Even Mr. Cody, who had been in many a battle, looked a little unsettled. Quickly, as if he had a little patch of quicksand to hurry over, he said, "Well, to tell you the truth, mam, it's Sitting Bull.

Now I know how you feel about the chief, but he knows those Black Hills like no one else. To him they are sacred land. He has risked his life for them many times."

Mama's face was flushed. "And in doing it he has taken the lives of others," she snapped.

"I don't ask that you forgive him, Mrs. James, just that you work with him. I don't think you will be sorry. Of, course, if you don't like it, we can just go back to the pictures."

I saw Mama was going to say no to my plan. "But Mama, you've said when you copy pictures, it's like someone else's heart beating in you."

Mama thought for a minute, and I was hopeful, but then she shook her head. "I don't believe the man can even speak English."

"And you don't speak Sioux, mam." Mr. Cody smiled. "Two Sky's boy can translate."

"I'm afraid it will never do, Mr. Cody."

"Well, mam, I wouldn't force you against your will. Just do the best you can with the backdrop."

After Mr. Cody left, I took a deep breath. I had to find a way to get Mama to know Sitting Bull, to let her see he wasn't just the evil man she thought him to be. I knew she might get very angry, but I felt I had to tell her about the medicine. "I have something to say, Mama," I began. "You know when you were sick and I gave you the medicine?"

"Yes, of course. It was after that I began to feel better."

"Mama," I said, my hand on her arm, my heart whirring like the wings of a flushed grouse, "it was Sitting Bull's medicine that tasted so bitter. He cured you."

Mama stared at me. "Miranda, how can you tell such a fib? It was medicine from the doctor."

"It's not a fib, Mama. The medicine came from Sitting Bull, not from the doctor. You can ask Two Sky."

Mama shook off my hand and said angrily, "You had no right to go behind my back, Miranda."

"But Mama," I cried, "you were dying."

"What if that man's black magic had made me worse?"

"But Mama, it didn't make you worse. It made you better!"

"It wasn't the medicine that made me better. The doctor said it was time passing. Now I don't want to hear another word about such nonsense."

I said no more words, but inside my head I thought them. I remembered how Mama had never been able to forgive her own mama and papa and ask their pardon. If she hadn't forgiven someone she loved, how would she ever forgive Sitting Bull?

CHAPTER NINE

Two days passed, and there was no more mention of Sitting Bull. Mama had been making sketches for the new backdrop of the Black Hills, with much crossing out and starting over. Finally, on the afternoon of the second day, she turned impatiently to me. In a peevish voice she said, "I've told Mr. Cody I'd try listening to Sitting Bull." Before I could say anything, she added, "But I won't like it." With Mama, making the best painting she could came before nearly everything else.

We had been with the Wild West Show for over three months, traveling from Chicago all along the East Coast and all the way up to Canada. Now we were in Michigan, with only a few more weeks before the show ended in St. Louis and closed for the season. I didn't want to think about saying good-bye to

115

Mr. Cody and Annie and Quick Fox and all the other friends I had made. Yet I was thinking more and more of our farm. The last time Mama and I had taken out the money box, we had been excited to find that there was enough money to live on the farm for a whole year. Mama had counted it twice to be sure. We had kept awake until late that night talking of how cozy we would be in the farmhouse in the Dakota winter and what we would plant when spring came.

In Detroit the posters announced: BUFFALO BILL IS KING OF THEM ALL. They promised: SEVERAL OF THE CELEBRATED WARRIORS LATELY AMONG THE HOSTILES, INCLUDING SITTING BULL AND 53 PAWNEE BRAVES, THIRTY NEW BUFFALOS AND 40 ELECTRIC AND CALCIUM LIGHTS.

The show took place on the east side of Detroit, in Recreation Park. People arrived on clanging streetcars and in crowded carriages. Although it was only early September, the leaves had a dusty, dull look. School had started, so there were fewer children hanging about the tents. The days were warm, but at night a cool breeze sneaked off the Detroit River. One night an early frost left the flowers in the park looking like wet mops.

It was in Detroit that Mama started the painting of the Black Hills. She sketched a background on the giant canvas, using some pictures Mr. Cody had given her, but all the important parts were waiting for Sitting Bull.

Sitting Bull arrived with Young Wolf. I greeted the chief in a whisper, afraid of Mama's anger if I appeared too friendly. Mama went pale at the sight of Sitting Bull. She tightened her lips into a straight line and narrowed her eyes. All her prettiness was gone. I knew she was thinking of Papa and his friends. Mama and Sitting Bull faced each other like two warriors.

When Mama turned to the backdrop, the chief said something in a soft voice to Young Wolf. Young Wolf whispered to me, "Sitting Bull says he would rather take on a whole army than your mother."

I saw Mama square her shoulders. She would not speak directly to Sitting Bull. She said to Young Wolf, "I am ready to listen to what he can tell me about the Black Hills. There will be no need to talk of anything else."

Sitting Bull nodded at Mama's words. He looked long and hard at her canvas. At last he said, "The *paha,* the hills, are higher, like small *he,* mountains. There are sudden rocks like jagged towers. Around the hills are fields of grass, buffalo grass, *pejihota,* and sagebrush."

As Mama listened to the chief's words, her face grew softer, her eyes opened wider, as though she were beginning to see what Sitting Bull was describing. She became busy with her brushes and paints. After a bit she said, "Young Wolf, ask him what he thinks of the canvas." She would not call Sitting Bull by name.

"The chief says you have forgotten the sagebrush. The sagebrush must be shown, he says. It is important to us, for we get our yellow dye and some of our medicines from it, and it protects us from evil spirits." Mama went to work again, but at the word "medicines" I saw her flinch. I was sure she was thinking about how she had taken Sitting Bull's medicine.

Sitting Bull, watching the painting, nodded, looking pleased. A few minutes later he interrupted Mama. "You must make the pine trees on the hills a darker green. That is why we call them Paha Sapa, Black Hills."

Mama darkened the green. This time she spoke

directly to Sitting Bull. "Are they dark enough?"

"*Sapa, sapa,*" he insisted.

Mama did not wait for Young Wolf to translate but mixed some more black with the green.

Sitting Bull smiled and nodded his head. I saw that he was eager to get everything right, to bring back the hills just as he remembered them. Mama and he were together in this, and I think Mama knew it, for she listened carefully to everything the chief said.

He pointed to the hills with his finger. "There," he said, "*wakpala,* a stream. And here, here, high in the hills, is the lake that is the mother of the stream. I have seen many animals there: elk, deer, wolf, coyote, and *capa.*"

Young Wolf could not think of the English word for *capa.* "It chews around trees so they fall down, and then the *capa* eat the bark."

"Beaver," I guessed.

Sitting Bull recognized the English word and nodded his head.

Something strange was happening. The chief's excitement was as catching as measles. The angry look was gone from Mama's face. I could tell she was excited from the way her brush flew as Sitting Bull's words made pictures for her.

Sitting Bull described a deep and clear lake, high in the hills. Mama painted the lake, making it a sky blue. Sitting Bull shook his head. He got up and strode toward the canvas. For a moment Mama looked frightened, but the chief was only pointing to the pine trees around the lake. He struggled to find a word. Young Wolf could not help him. Mama saw what he wanted. "The reflection of the trees in the water," she said. "The water should be a green-blue. Of course, why didn't I think of that myself?"

It was time for the afternoon show, but Sitting Bull did not want to leave. "Young Wolf," Mama said, "tell him I promise I will only finish some trees and do nothing more until he returns." I could see the chief did not want to leave even the trees in Mama's hands without his being there, but finally he turned away.

Young Wolf and Quick Fox and Small Snow and I followed him, for it was time to get ready for our trip in the Deadwood coach. Sitting Bull told Young Wolf to say to me, "I am glad your mother has a brush in her hand instead of a gun, or I would not be safe."

After that he laughed heartily and went on his way.

The next morning there was the same disagreeable feeling when Mama and Sitting Bull met, but again, as soon as they started to work, Mama's anger was put aside and I began to hope they would become friends, or if not friends, at least not enemies.

"All last night I dreamed of birds," Sitting Bull said. "Once a *wagnuka,* a woodpecker, saved my life. I was asleep in the woods. The Great Spirit sent the *wagnuka* to awaken me. It told me to stay very still. A grizzly bear came and stood over me. I was quiet and the bear went away. There should be birds in the Paha Sapa. There are hawks that fly over the hills and *wablosa,* red-winged blackbirds, near the stream." He turned to me. "We must have the *jialepa,* the meadowlark with its song like an Indian flute. Your daughter will tell you how it must be painted. It is her bird as well."

Mama looked at me in surprise. "How does he know that?" she demanded. "Have you been talking with him, Miranda?"

"Only just a little." I tried to excuse myself. Hastily, I went on to describe the meadowlark while Mama painted it. "A little more yellow under its chin," I said.

Mama shrugged. "Here is the brush. You color the bird." So I became a part of the Black Hills.

Late in the afternoons Mama would stop working on the backdrop and send Sitting Bull away. "The light is not right," she said. "For painting you must have a strong light." As soon as Mama was gone, Sitting Bull returned, often bringing the other Indians with him. He pointed out the animals and birds. They stood in front of the canvas for an hour at a time, often with sad looks on their faces.

"Are they unhappy with Mama's painting?" I asked Mr. Cody.

"No, indeed. Your mama has made the painting of the Black Hills so real, the Indians look at it and grieve for what they have lost. They are saddened, for they know the land in the painting is lost to them forever."

I often heard the Indians use the word *wakan* when they looked at the backdrop of the Black Hills. I asked Young Wolf, "What does that word mean?"

"They are calling the hills holy," Young Wolf said. "Great storms come to the hills with thunder and lightning. Such storms are not to be found anywhere else."

Sitting Bull was hard to satisfy, so it was not until we reached Columbus, Ohio, that the backdrop was finally finished. As Mama laid down her brush and turned away from the canvas, she took a deep breath and said to Young Wolf, "Please tell Sitting Bull that I have appreciated his help." It was the first time she had called him by name. I knew the words that were coming were hard for her to say. "It is the chief's love of the land that has made the Black Hills come alive for me. His descriptions made all the difference."

Even before Young Wolf translated her words, the chief could tell that Mama had said a friendly thing. He reached into his pocket and took out a pebble. "It once lay along the shore of the lake you painted," Sitting Bull said to Mama. "I have carried it with me for many years." He handed it to Mama. At first she did not want to take it, but at last she thanked the chief, and slipping it into the pocket of her apron, she hurried away.

The backdrop was displayed behind the Deadwood coach. When the audience first saw it, there were shouts of pleasure and much applause. As pleased as the audience was, I had had no idea how well Mama and Sitting Bull had succeeded in making the Black Hills real until that afternoon. As the coach rolled along with all of us inside, the Indians attacked. This time they did not smile and wink at us as they usually did. They rode their ponies hard, and their war whoops were loud. My scream was louder than usual, for I was truly frightened. When Mr. Cody and the soldiers stormed out, the Indians took longer than usual to fall down from their horses and play dead. I think the sight of the Black Hills made them think of the days when they were real warriors, of days when they were the ones to win the battles.

CHAPTER TEN

It was October when we reached St. Louis, the last stop of Buffalo Bill's Wild West Show for the season. Sitting Bull seemed ready to leave the show, and he departed several days ahead of us. I believe the sight of the Black Hills on Mama's backdrop had set him to thinking of land where he would be able to leave behind streetcars and crowds of people. As a parting gift Mr. Cody gave Sitting Bull the gray horse the chief had ridden in the parades. He also gave him a white Stetson hat like the one he himself wore. Everyone was sorry to see Sitting Bull leave. Except Mama.

I could not persuade her. "Mama, you and Sitting Bull worked together. You said yourself that because of Sitting Bull's help, the backdrop of the Black Hills was the best painting you ever did."

"It was my job to make the best painting I could, Miranda. It had nothing to do with how I felt about Sitting Bull."

"But Mama," I pleaded, "why must you still be angry with him? You once told me that it's a terrible thing not to forgive."

"Don't throw my words back at me, Miranda. That was different." Mama looked at the portrait of Papa. "How can I forget Sitting Bull killed your papa?" Her face clouded over. "Sitting Bull should be in prison for what he did."

Much as I loved Mama, I saw at last that we were different. Mama could not climb out of herself, and I could. I could understand how Quick Fox or Mr. Cody or Sitting Bull felt. I could imagine being them, happy at what made them happy and sad at what made them sad. What bothered me most was that there would always be a part of me that I couldn't share with Mama.

When I went to say good-bye to Sitting Bull, I wished Mama had come with me, but I knew it would be useless to ask her. I thought Sitting Bull was disappointed as well, but he only asked Young Wolf to tell me, "Your mother has not long to wait for her revenge upon me. I feel it will soon come."

His words gave me shivers. "Young Wolf," I said, "ask Sitting Bull where he will go when he leaves the show."

"Back to the Standing Rock Agency," Sitting Bull said. That was less than a hundred miles from Fort Lincoln and our farm. I quickly resolved I would not tell Mama that Sitting Bull would be so close to us. I was afraid it might spoil the farm for her.

"What will you do at the Standing Rock Agency?" I asked.

Sitting Bull sighed. "I will become a farmer, tied to the land like a *sunka*, a dog, tied to a tree with a rope." He looked about his tepee. "Here," he said, "you must have this." He handed me the hawk's wing feather I had seen him use to fan himself. "It is from a hawk that once soared over the Paha Sapa. It is a great gift to be able to go where you wish. I pass that gift on to you, for it is too late for me."

The hawk's wing seemed to flutter in my hands. Quickly, I ran to our tent and hid the chief's gift in my trunk. The next day Sitting Bull left the show for the Standing Rock Agency.

When it was our turn to leave, I spent my last

afternoon just wandering around the show trying to memorize everything so I could recall it when I was back in Dakota. I could still hardly believe all the things I had seen and done that summer and all the friends I had made.

Mr. Cody was so pleased with the work Mama had done, he said to her, "Mrs. James, promise me you'll join us when the show opens next spring. We'll open in New York City, mam, and I'll tell you a secret I haven't told the others. I have a mind to pack the whole show up this year or next and take it to Europe—London and Paris and Rome. What do you say to that?" He smiled at me. "What a lesson in geography that would be for Miranda!"

Mama's eyes lit up. "It would be, and I would give anything to see the famous works of art in those great cities. But first Miranda and I must go back to the farm. Then we'll think about the future."

I said good-bye to Buck Taylor and Con Groner. I threw my arms around Annie Oakley and dared to give Mr. Cody a kiss on the cheek.

Hardest of all was saying good-bye to Quick Fox. Her family was all going to join the show again in the spring. Now that Sitting Bull had left, Young Wolf was quiet and more watchful again. Somehow Quick Fox had learned Mr. Cody was thinking of taking the show to Europe, and she was full of gossip about the kings and queens. "Queen Victoria wears black all the time because her husband, Prince Albert, died. She's tiny and fat as a pigeon. Her son, Edward, has more lady friends than you can count on two hands." Small Snow was gathering brightly colored autumn leaves. Now she ran to hug me and make me promise I would do all I could to coax Mama to come back.

As anxious as I was to return to the farm, I was sorry to leave. I walked with my friends one last time around the show. We were all quiet, even Quick Fox, and for once Small Snow stayed close by.

"Where will you go now?" I asked Quick Fox, thinking of how we would be on our very own farm.

"We'll probably have to spend the winter on the reservation," she answered sadly. "I hate the reservation. The teachers think Indians are stupid, and the government agents think we're beggars because we get government money. They forget we get the money because they took our land. What they pay us isn't near enough."

"I wish you could come and visit me," I said. I

didn't want to think of her on the reservation. "I'll write to you. Will you promise to write back?"

"Sure. Then you can tell me if you're coming back to the show."

We hugged, and Quick Fox ran off. I stood watching until she had disappeared into the Indian village.

Mama and I packed our trunks for the last time. As we were leaving our tent, I saw that Mama had left Sitting Bull's pebble behind. I made some excuse and ran back to catch the pebble up and put it in my pocket. All those years, when I hadn't known Sitting Bull, I had hated him. It had taken only a few months of knowing him to let my hate go.

We took the steamboat from St. Louis up the Missouri to Fort Lincoln. There were rumors that the fort would soon be closed. Now that we finally had enough money to live in the farmhouse and grow vegetables, there was no guarantee that anyone would be around to buy them. But Mama said we were not to worry, there would always be the Wild West Show to return to.

On the way to the fort, the boat passed very close to the Standing Rock Agency, where Sitting Bull was. The land around the agency was as flat and dry as a sheet of brown wrapping paper. There were few trees. It was nothing like the Black Hills. I thought Mama had her wish. If Sitting Bull could no longer ride across the prairie and the hills, if he could no longer hunt buffalo or move his tepee where he wanted to, he was in prison.

How different it was for us. After we greeted our old friends at the fort, a wagon carried us along with our furniture and trunks to our farm. The leaves had dropped from the cottonwood tree and the lilac bush, but the creek ran clear and fast. The Dakota winds rattled the windows, but Mama and I were snug in our little house. On the morning of the first snow I saw a meadowlark, its feathers puffed out for warmth. I wondered if there were meadowlarks at the Standing Rock Agency and if Sitting Bull would see one and think of me as I thought of him.

AUTHOR'S NOTE

While writing this book, I traveled along the Missouri River to Fort Lincoln, visiting General Custer's home and Laundresses' Row. In Montana I walked the Little Big Horn battleground. At the Buffalo Bill Museum in Cody, Wyoming, I saw the Deadwood coach. The location of the true burial ground of Sitting Bull is in dispute, but some believe it is in the vicinity of the Standing Rock Agency in North Dakota. Sitting Bull was killed there on a cold winter day in 1890 by Indian police working for the United States government. It was said that Sitting Bull was threatening to leave the reservation. When I was there, the grave believed by many to be Sitting Bull's was difficult to find, the only direction a worn, hand-lettered sign leaning against a tree.

GLORIA WHELAN is a poet and an award-winning writer who has written many books for young readers, including The Indian School; Once on This Island, which won the 1996 Great Lakes Book Award; and Farewell to the Island. She lives with her husband, Joseph, in the woods of northern Michigan.